MW00460268

The girl who Never Was

The girl Who Never Was

Wendy griffin

Charleston, SC
www.PalmettoPublishing.com

The Girl Who Never Was

Copyright © 2022 by Wendy Griffin

All rights reserved.

No portion of this book may be reproduced, stored in a retrieval system, or transmitted in any form by any means-electronic, mechanical, photocopy, recording, or other-except for brief quotations in printed reviews, without prior permission of the author.

First Edition

Hardcover ISBN: 978-1-63837-578-4
Paperback ISBN: 978-1-63837-577-7
eBook ISBN: 978-1-63837-576-0

TABLE OF CONTENTS

Chapter 1

A NEW HOME

It was a clear night. Maple had fallen asleep. In her day she must have been a beautiful sight. She was bred for racing. I could just see her—a big bay mare on the racetrack. But now she was a broodmare in foal, and we were resting under the stars. I was lying on her back looking up at the stars, my head on her rump and my feet crossed on her neck. I felt her shift her weight from one hind foot to the other as she slept. The stars were out, but there was no moon.

I heard the sound of footsteps coming toward Maple. She didn't seem to mind. There were ten mares in this pasture, and all were bred. But it wasn't one of the other mares; it was Lucky. As he came closer, I could see his massive figure. He stood sixteen hands tall, with muscles bulging everywhere. He's the sire for all the foals in this pasture.

Lucky came over to Maple and pushed me off her with his nose. Maple stomped her foot in disapproval.

"Hey, Lucky! You didn't have to do that." He looked at me as if he knew what I was saying. "Come on, Lucky. Time to put you back in the barn. Tomorrow is my first day at my new school. I hope I do OK.

What do you think, Lucky?" He just nudged me toward the barn with his nose.

Through the darkness came another sound, a rustling. I couldn't see a thing; it was so dark. Lucky and I stopped and listened for a minute before Jim came running. Jim is a black-and-white border collie that I found one day in the pasture. He was half starved and thin as a rail. It took awhile, but he looks good now. The vet said he was about a year old. Jim is a great dog. He and Lucky are my best friends.

As we headed to the barn, Lucky and Jim acted a little restless. I couldn't see far ahead, but I trusted their instincts. Once we got closer, I could see car lights in front of the barn. We stopped and watched for a little bit.

All I could tell was that it was a police car. My parents sometimes came looking for me when social services came around. They didn't like me at the house, but they also didn't want any trouble from social services. Between my dad and my brother beating me up, I got fed up and ran away.

I stayed in this barn for about two weeks before anyone even knew I was there. But when they found out, they called the police. An officer came and picked me up and took me to the police station. And that's where I met Lieutenant Glen. He took a liking to me. When he saw all the bruises, he asked me what was going on. I told him about my dad and brother, and I asked him if I could stay at Hickory Oaks Farm. I said I'd stay out of trouble. I did *not* want to stay in an orphanage. He talked to the owners of the farm, and they said it was OK for now. Now I was scared the officer was here to pick me up again, so I was hesitant to go on. Lucky, Jim, and I stayed back, out of sight, for a long while, but the officer wasn't going anywhere. We couldn't stay out here forever, so we headed to the barn.

I opened the gate to walk through, with Lucky and Jim behind me. The officer approached us. Lucky was a big stallion, and when he's upset he looks even bigger. Lucky stomped his foot and got between me and the officer. Jim was standing beside us, growling. Neither of them liked this man.

I told the officer that I needed to put Lucky up (away in his stall). Lucky didn't care much for strangers. I led Lucky into the barn and told him to calm down.

The officer introduced himself. "Scout, my name is Bobby Carson. Lieutenant Glen said to come by and check on you. He wanted to know if you had all you need for school tomorrow."

"I think I have everything I need, but why are you here so late at night?"

"There've been reports of some horse stealing. Have any gone missing around here?"

"No," I said. "I just checked; everyone is accounted for in this barn. You need to go talk to Gary, the trainer over at the other barn. But he won't be there this late. I don't go over to that barn very often; this is a big farm. At any one time, there could be as many as a hundred horses here, all together. This is just the breeding area—nothing here but young horses and broodmares and two stallions."

"Well, if you hear of anything unusual, please let me know."

Bobby Carson is a short, chubby man with a sweet smile. He couldn't have been much older than thirty, with blond hair and blue eyes. But there was just something suspicious about him...I guessed it was just my nerves. I didn't know why Jim and Lucky didn't like him, but I followed their lead. I always trusted my animals over anything else.

After the officer left, I went inside to get things ready for the first day of school the next day. Boy, did I hate school. I had to go; that's the way it was. It would be my first day in seventh grade and at a new school. I hoped all would go well.

Lieutenant Glen worked it out with the owners so I could live on this farm. They were never here, always traveling to horse shows all over the country. There was a little bunk room in the barn fixed up for me. I had to feed horses and help Jessie and Mae look after the broodmares and foals on this side of the farm, which is a little over two thousand acres, or so I was told.

It was such a nice night that Jim and I decided to sleep on the back side of the barn in the hay so we could see the stars and look out over the pastures. I loved it here. I'd never been scared to be alone; I'd always found it peaceful.

Jessie and Mae would be here first thing in the morning. Jessie is a young Black man in his twenties, and Mae, his wife, is about the same age. They would bring me some breakfast in the morning, like always. I couldn't make it without them. They're the reason the owners let me stay. Mae wanted me to live with them, but too many people wouldn't like that, and I didn't want to cause any trouble. And besides, I did like it right here.

***

The next morning came quick. Jessie tried to wake me from a deep sleep. I didn't usually sleep that hard, so Jessie was fussing. "Wake up, girl! You've got to go to school now. Get up!"

"OK, Jessie. OK. I'm up."

Jim was licking my face, and Jessie was pulling on my arm. I got up and moved around to start feeding the horses, but Jessie said, "I've already fed these guys. Now, you go get ready for school."

Jessie handed me my breakfast, which was a bacon-and-egg sandwich and some orange juice. It tasted really good this morning. It was going to be a nice, warm day, and that breakfast was a good start. Jim was jumping around, not knowing what all the fuss was about. I hadn't left Jim since I got him.

"Jessie, you going to look after Jim for me today? You know I've never left him before."

"I'll keep him with me all day. He'll be fine. The bus driver said he'd pick you up around seven, so go get ready—it's after six now!"

"OK, Jessie. OK! I'm going."

Mae met me at the bunk room with some clean clothes and a big smile. "Come on, girl. Get your things together. It's getting late."

"Thank you, Mae. I'm going."

I was ready in plenty of time. I didn't know what all the fuss was about. The bus pulled up, and I reluctantly got on. Jim sat by Jessie, and I watch them through the bus window until I couldn't see them anymore.

School was OK. I just went to class and did what I had to do. I like staying in the back of the classroom and out of sight. All went well, and it was over at three o'clock. In my daydreams throughout the day, I saw myself getting off the bus and running to the barn.

The farm is about one-and-a-half miles from the school. When I did get off the bus at the farm, Jim came running to me, and Lucky was standing at the gate to the pasture. It was so good to see Jim.

As I walked in the barn, Jessie and Mae were grooming horses. "Scout, how was school?" Mae asked.

"It was fine…just like a caged animal in the zoo," I replied.

"Did you meet some new friends today?" Jessie asked.

"No, I didn't try. I just wanted the day to be over with so I could get back here to see you and Mae and, most of all, Jim." Lucky was about to knock down the gate outside when I didn't come speak to him. "I also missed Lucky too. I'm coming, Lucky. Don't break down the gate." I walked out of the barn to see Lucky, with Jim walking right behind me. Mae looked at Jessie and said, "She's not happy going to that school, Jessie."

"Mae, she has to go for her own good. I know she doesn't like it, but there is nothing we can do about it."

"I just hate seeing her like this, Jessie."

"She'll be all right. Just give her some time." Jessie walked off, leading a young mare back to her stall.

Mae said to herself, "I sure hope you're right."

***

"Lucky, how was your day?" I was sad I hated school. Lucky just pushed me with his nose, glad to see me. "Go on out to the pasture, and see your mares. I'll be out later."

Lucky turned and walked out into the field. He was such a pretty, big sorrel, with a flax mane and tail. He was so pretty that I couldn't take my eyes off of him as he walked out into the field. He was so proud and sure of himself. I thought to myself, I wish I could be that confident.

***

The next couple of weeks at school went well. All my teachers were nice to me, and my grades were good.

The principal was a friend of Lieutenant Glen and knew about my situation. He told me I could use the washer and dryer at the school if I needed to wash my clothes. He also said that if I wanted to use the showers, that would be all right too. I thanked him and told him I would let him know when I needed to use them.

The weather had really been good. At night you could feel the air was getting cooler, but the days were still nice. I hated cold weather, but I knew it would be here soon.

Jim's hair was already getting thick, and Lucky already looked like a woolly booger. I didn't know where all that hair came from. Lucky's hair is slick as glass in the summertime, then all at once he's woolly.

I just hoped winter wouldn't be a long one. It was getting dark earlier in the day, and the nights were getting longer. So winter was on its way, and there was nothing I could do about it.

Homework was hard to do sometimes—when all the help I had was Jim (even though he was the best dog ever) and Lucky. Math was *not* our favorite subject. But everything else was OK. I would have algebra the next semester, and there was no way I'd be able to do it. Math was hard enough. Oh well. I'd deal with that when it happens. The next day would be Saturday, and the weather was supposed to be great—close to seventy, which for this time of year is great.

Officer Carson would be coming tomorrow, bringing his wife, Karen, and his little girl, Carol. He came by one day last week while I was at school and told Jessie he was coming this Saturday. Jessie told him I never go anywhere but to school and back to this old barn and then said, "I think Scout is a wild animal at heart. No one really knows what she's all about."

Carson looked at Jessie and said, "What do you mean?"

"Well, she doesn't want to harm anybody, but she would love just to be with the animals. The horses and that dog, Jim, look after her like she's one of them. I've never seen anything like it before." Carson said, "Saturday I'm bringing my wife and little girl out here to see Scout. I think she needs to see more people. Besides, Lieutenant Glen said to keep an eye on her."

"Well, don't you hurt her in any way because I would do anything for her. She's a good kid." Jessie walked away, saying to himself, "I don't like that man. He is up to no good."

* * *

Early Saturday morning, Jim, Lucky, and I, after eating our breakfast, fed the other animals. There were about thirty mares split between three different pastures. There were twenty stalls in the barn. Most of the stalls were for when the mares have their foals or are sick or hurt. The owners kept two stallions. One was Lucky, the big sorrel they pasture breed, and the other was a big bay stallion by the name of Hank. He was a nice horse but didn't like too much attention, unlike Lucky. But boy was he pretty. They used him mostly for breeding outside mares (ones that someone else owned and brought here to be bred).

This was just one of two barns on this farm. The farm was divided into two sections. This section was the breeding area and had around six hundred acres. On the other side of the farm, there was another five hundred acres used for boarding and training horses.

The people that owned this place were the Hunters. They didn't have any children and stayed out of the country most of the time selling or showing horses. Gary was their trainer, and he stayed at the other barn most of the time. I saw him only once in a while.

There was a big bunk house at the other barn for everyone who worked over there. We had a small bunk room at this barn so someone—usually Jessie—could be here during foaling time. I was using that room for right now.

Jessie came into work and saw that all of the animals were already fed. He looked at me and said, "Why do I bother coming to work? You've already fed everyone. Well, let's get these stalls cleaned before that Officer Carson gets here."

"Why do you not like him, Jessie? Lucky and Jim act a little funny around him also."

"I don't know, Scout. There is just something about him. I can't rightly put my finger on it, but there's something about him. I'm going to stay here while they're here, just in case."

"That's fine with me, Jessie. You know, you and Mae are the best thing that's happened to me, and I respect your opinion. And besides that, I'd starve to death without the both of you."

"I guess you'd get pretty hungry." Jessie had a big smile on his face. What a wonderful person Jessie is, I told myself.

Jessie turned to walk away, then looked back at Scout and said, "Scout, you're a good friend to Mae and me also. You know that, don't you?"

"I do. And thank you, Jessie, for everything."

After cleaning stalls I took a quick shower in the wash stall where we wash horses. It was the only place to take a shower, but it at least had hot water. Jessie had said to never take a shower there unless he or Mae was around. He was worried that someone would come in when I was in there and would just walk in on me. Well, I told him Jim wouldn't let anyone do that. But it was best to listen to Jessie.

* * *

It was about nine o'clock, and the Carsons would be here soon.

After what Jessie said about Officer Carson, I was not looking forward to the visit. What if he was up to something? What if he was not a nice person and Lucky, Jim, and Jessie were right? I was ready for this visit to be over.

Lucky hadn't gone out to the pasture and was standing by the gate. He knew something different was going to happen. Jim hadn't left my side. He was still wet because he wouldn't even let me take a shower without him standing right there. So I bathed him too. At least he was clean. Jim didn't like little children much, so I hoped he was good with Carol. I didn't know how old she was. I never thought to ask Officer Carson.

It was turning out to be a beautiful fall day: the leaves starting to change, the sun bright, and not a cloud in the sky. I couldn't ask for a nicer day.

At around ten o'clock, a black SUV came down the driveway.

Jessie said to me, "That's them. I feel it in my bones."

"I don't get it, Jessie. Why do you feel that way?"

"I don't know, little one. It's just how I feel."

The SUV pulled up and stopped, and the Carsons got out. All three looked so much alike that they made me smile. Jessie had to smile also. Officer Carson's wife was just a little shorter than him but just as chubby. Carol, the daughter, was just a shorter version of her parents.

They brought me a winter coat, which was great because I didn't have one. I showed them the farm, and Carol loved it. Officer Carson said he would bring Carol out one Saturday and let her spend the day if it was OK with me. She was a sweet girl, and I liked her a lot.

After the tour of the farm, they wanted to take me to lunch in town. I didn't get to eat out very often. I asked Jessie if it was all right, and he said yes. Officer Carson gave a snide look when I asked Jessie, and Jessie gave him the same look back. Well, one thing was for sure: they did *not* like each other.

We went to a restaurant that had a salad bar and a full buffet. I had never seen so much food. We ate, talked, and laughed for two hours. Then, I gathered scraps for Jim before we left.

On the way back to the farm, Officer Carson asked me to call him "Bobby." He said all his friends called him that. He said he hoped we all could be friends. I told him I'd like that myself—even though I didn't think Jessie, Jim, or Lucky would ever go for that.

When we got back to the farm, Jessie was waiting for us. He just didn't trust Officer Carson. The Carsons left, and I told Jessie that Officer Carson wanted me to call him "Bobby." Jessie didn't say anything, but I could tell he didn't like that at all.

But one thing was for sure: Jim loved the scraps I got him.

Chapter 2

WILLY

They wanted me to play on the basketball team and volleyball team at school. I tried to tell the coach that I didn't have a ride after the buses leave in the afternoon. She said she would work something out if I played. I thought I'd like it, but I would have to talk to Jessie and see.

There was a new kid at school. He was an American Indian. I didn't know much about him because, like me, he kept to himself most of the time. We didn't have any other American Indians at the school, so he does stand out. He sat at my table when we ate lunch. His name was Willy. I didn't know his last name. I told him I was called Scout. That ended our talk. There are two other kids who sat at the same table at lunch. Their names were Cindy and Max. None of us felt like we fit in at this school, and that's the only thing we had in common.

Willy was a small, thin boy, with big brown eyes and dark brown skin. He looked a little small for his age. Cindy was also small and thin, with blonde hair and blue eyes, and she looked scared all the time. Max was a big boy, with black hair and hazel eyes, and he thought everyone hated him. Then there was me, with long, stringy brown hair that never looked brushed no matter how much I brushed it. I have green eyes, and it would have been nice if I were a little taller. None of us talked much, but we seemed to like each other's company at lunch.

Willy had been at the school a week now, and the only thing he had said was his name. Cindy, I thought, had a bad time at home. She often had bruises, and she cried a lot. The other kids gave her a hard time.

Max, I thought, lived on the street. He smelled bad most of the time. I wanted to tell him he could take a shower in the gym, but I didn't know how to tell him without hurting his feelings. He was too big for the other children to give him a hard time to his face.

Not one of us made good grades, and we didn't ask questions in class. We just wanted each day to be over. But I'm glad I had them to sit with at lunch. The next day would be basketball and volleyball try-outs. I had been really thinking about going to them. I'd talk to Jessie and Mae about it tonight. But the only problem was I'd have to talk to my parents to get the money for my uniforms. I didn't know if any of this was worth it or not.

*＊＊

I decided to walk back to the farm that afternoon from school. It was only a short distance, and I needed the time to think.

While on my way, I ran into Willy. "Hi, Willy. What are you doing walking?"

"I always walk to and from school. What're *you* doing walking this way? I've never seen you walk this way before." Willy looked a little nervous.

"I'm thinking about trying out for basketball and volleyball, so I decided to walk back to think about it. How far do you have to walk, Willy?"

Willy, looking a little unsure, said, "Only a little less than a mile. I live too close to ride the bus. Where do you live, Scout? "I was surprised; I had never thought about it, and no one had ever asked me that before. "I can't talk about that right now. Maybe I could show you one day if I get to stay."

Willy looked like he understood and said, "I know what you mean. I go from place to place also."

Just then, a police car pulled up, and Willy got really nervous.

"It's OK, Willy. That's just Officer Carson." I turned to Carson. "Hello, Bobby. What are you doing here?" I turned around to look for Willy, but he was already way up the road.

"I could ask you the same thing, Scout," Carson said. "What are you doing walking? Did you miss the bus?" I couldn't help but look puzzled. Why was that any of his business?

"No, I just wanted to walk. I have something I wanted to think about."

"Who was that boy, Scout?" Carson looked at me strangely.

"He's a boy from school. I don't know much about him, but I do like him." Carson, still looking a little strange, asked, "Well, what do you have to think about that would make you walk back to the farm?"

"Oh, not much, just something I want to talk to Jessie and Mae about."

"You in trouble?" Carson asked.

"No, not in trouble. Just some school stuff...I want to thank you again for this coat. It sure is warm," I said, trying to change the subject.

"Do you want a ride, or are you still thinking?" I looked around one more time to see where Willy was, but he was nowhere to be seen. And it was getting late. So I got in the car, and we drove to the farm. On the way, Carson kept asking about what was going on and why I was walking. I wanted to tell him it was none of his business, but, instead, I just told him everything was all right. But I felt uneasy around him for the first time. I remembered what Jessie said: "There is just something about him." Carson went on. "I could help you if you just tell me what's going on with you? Does that boy have anything to do with it?"

"No," I said. "I told you everything is fine."

We got back to the farm, and Jessie wasn't happy. He saw me in the police car and just knew something was wrong. "Girl, you are late. Why are you in that police car?"

I could tell this wasn't going to be good. Jessie had never gotten upset with me before.

Bobby got out of the car and told Jessie, "I saw her walking down the road, and I stopped to give her a ride. I hope that's OK. I didn't think that would be a problem."

"No, that's all right. I just worry about her. She's so young to be on her own like she is." Jessie started to calm down some.

Jim came running out of the barn; he wasn't used to me being late either. As I pet him, Carson got in his car and drove away.

Jessie frowned at me and said, "You know I don't trust that man. Why were you in the car with him?"

Before I could answer, Mae came out of the barn, leading Lucky. When she saw me, she turned him loose. Lucky came over and nudged me like he was mad at me too.

Mae looked at Jessie and said, "Leave her be, Jessie." Mae walked over and put her arm around me and asked, "How was your day, Scout?"

I started telling her about my day—about basketball, volleyball, and Willy. Jessie listened as we talked, then he walked over and told me that he was sorry for fussing at me. Then he smiled and asked, "Do you want something to eat? Miss Mae brought you some veggie soup and cornbread." I hadn't thought about it, but when he mentioned soup and cornbread, I realized I was starving.

After eating I helped feed the horses and put them up. Before Jessie left, he said, "Scout, stay in the barn. It's going to storm tonight." I told him I would. Jim was acting like it might storm also. He didn't like storms. Jessie said he would let me know in the morning about the sports thing, and that was all right with me because I was tired of thinking about it anyway.

* * *

That night after doing my homework, it started raining. It was getting late. The wind was blowing, and the horses were restless. All of a sudden, there was a bright strike of lightning and then thunder that shook the barn like a saltshaker. Jim and I both jumped. Lightning that bright and thunder so close behind it meant that the storm was right overhead. I liked a good storm but not when it was that close.

Jim and I were in the hayloft inside the barn. The little bunk room was so small and dark; I liked it out in the hayloft better, plus I loved the sweet smell of hay.

Then there was another lightning strike and thunder so loud I could feel it all through my body. The rain was coming down so hard, and the wind was blowing the rain into sheets of water coming down.

It was coming down so hard that it would even scare the spirits. I believed in spirits—spirits in live things and spirits of the dead. Jessie said that was what made me different from other folks. Jim and I huddled in the stall with Lucky, along with any spirits that wanted to join us.

At first light, if you wanted to call it light, it was so foggy you couldn't see your hand in front of your face. After feeding the horses in the barn, we went out to check the mares in the pastures. There were three pastures with horses in them. At the first pasture, all the mares came right up. These were all the mares that were bred. They all looked fine, but Maple looked a little frazzled but OK. I fed these mares and went on to the next pasture. Only three mares came up when I called, even though there were ten mares that usually stayed in this field. None of these mares were bred. I decided to bring them inside until I could find the others. In the next field, all eight fillies were just standing, waiting to eat. I was most worried about these girls because they were just yearlings, but they all looked fine. Jim and I went back to the pasture where the missing horses were supposed to be. We went into the pasture to look for them, but the fog was so dense that it was hard to see. I didn't remember the fog ever being this bad. It took awhile to get to the back side of the field, but we still didn't see any horses.

After a while we came across some tire tracks. We followed the tracks a ways until we saw the fence was down. I told Jim to go back to the barn to get Jessie. He would be there by now. I headed to where the fence was down. It had been a cold morning, but I hadn't noticed till now. My feet were wet, and the chill was running up my body.

* * *

Jim went running to the barn when Jessie and Mae drove in. They saw him running into the barn, as if a bobcat were after him. Mae looked at Jessie and said, "Something's wrong, Jessie."

"Mae, you're right. Something's not right. And where is Scout?"

Jim was jumping around like a fool dog. Mae noticed the pasture gate. "Jessie, the gate is open. You think Scout went out to check something?"

"Jim, go to Scout now." Jessie didn't have to say it twice; Jim was on the run. Mae and Jessie jumped back in the truck and headed out into the field behind him.

"I'm worried, Jessie. It's not like Scout to do this."

"I just hope she didn't go and get hurt or something." "She's going to be late for school if we don't find her soon."

Jessie said a little angrily, "She didn't do this to be late for school, Mae. Don't judge her before you know what's going on."

"Jessie, I feel something bad has happened. I feel it in my bones."

"I do too, Mae, but let's not get all worked up till we know what has happened."

Jim took off through the open gate at a flat-out run. Jessie tried to keep up the best he could. "As muddy and foggy as it is, we're going to have a hard time keeping up with Jim. I can't hardly see him."

Mae just kept her eyes on Jim. At one point, she lost sight of him and yelled out the window for him to slow down and come back. He did as he was told, even though he didn't like it.

Jessie looked at Mae and said, "Where is that dog going?"

"I don't know, Jessie, but he is going like a bat out of hell."

* * *

After sending Jim back for Jessie, I headed to the cut fence for a closer look. The skies were still cloudy, but the storms were gone. As I got closer to the fence, I saw three people in the distance and yelled, "Who are you? What are you doing here?"

"Scout, run!" One of the figures in the distance started running toward me. "Scout, run!" As this small figure got closer, I recognized the voice.

"Willy, is that you?"

"Scout, run!"

A chill ran down my back. "Willy, what's wrong?" I yelled.

"Go, Scout! Run!"

At that moment I heard a loud bang, and Willy hit the ground, face-first.I froze for a moment, then turned and started running as fast as I could. I ran and cried so hard that I didn't see Jim running to me, and I ran right over him and fell on the ground. Jessie and Mae arrived and thought I was hurt. They both jumped out of the truck to check on me. Jessie asked if I was all right, but all I could do was point. I was holding Jim and crying and rocking back and forth.

Mae walked toward the cut fence, and Jessie heard her let out a loud scream. "Mae, what is it?"

"Jessie, come quick, please!"

The fog was still pretty thick, and Jessie had to get close to see what on earth was going on. And then he saw this small body lying in a pool of blood.

Mae, crying, said, "Jessie, who would do this?

Who, Jessie...who could do such a thing?"

"Mae...I don't know."

Mae couldn't stop crying. Jessie couldn't help it either, and tears flowed down his cheeks.

Jessie held Mae for a moment and then said, "We need to get Scout back to the barn and call the police. I'll stay here. You go get Scout and go to the barn and call the police."

"What if they come back, Jessie?"

"I'll be OK. Now go."

As Mae was heading back to the truck, she stopped to get me. I was still sitting on the ground holding Jim and crying.

"Come on, Scout. We have to get help. Please, Scout, come on." Mae was begging. "Come on, Scout. Get in the truck. We have to go call the police." I kept saying, "We can't just leave Jessie, Mae." I was still crying hard. "Those people might hurt him."

"Come on, Scout. We have to get help." Mae helped me to my feet and led me to the truck. Mae had never driven this truck this fast before. I held on so hard that I had to stop crying. Jim bounced around like a rag doll. He wasn't sure what was going on.

When we got back to the barn, Mae ran in to use the phone to call for help. She called 911 and, as fast as she could, told them what was going on—or at least what she thought was going on. When she got off the phone, she went looking for me. She went into the hallway of the barn just in time to see me jump on Lucky and head back out into the pasture.

Mae called out, "Where are you going, Scout?"

"Jessie can't stay out there by himself; I have to go help him."

"Be careful, girl!" Mae said, knowing that there was nothing else she could do.

I knew I couldn't push Lucky hard; the ground was wet, and it was still foggy. As we came up on Jessie, standing over Willy, we had to stop short. I got off Lucky and walk the rest of the way, with Lucky and Jim close behind.

Jessie looked at me and said, "Do you know him?"

All I could do was nod my head.

"Where do you know him from?"

I couldn't talk. Tears were rolling down my face. I couldn't even see. Jessie grabbed me and held me tight. I couldn't stop crying.

A police car pulled up, and Mae got out and ran to Jessie and me. Officer Carson got out and started walking toward us, but Lucky got all bowed up and stood between Carson and the rest of us. I looked at Lucky. "What's up, Lucky?" He just flattened his ears and would not let Carson near us. Carson stood back. "Scout, I need to talk to you. Mae said you saw everything. Lieutenant Glen is on his way." Lucky wouldn't let him get close at all. "Jessie, I need to see that boy."

"Scout, get Lucky away so he can come see."

"OK, Jessie. Come on, Lucky." He was reluctant but did as I asked. Carson looked at the body—Willy's body, the boy I was walking with just yesterday. I was hoping he would be a friend, but then he was gone. He looked so small lying there.

Lieutenant Glen drove up and got out of his car. He looked at Willy and talked to Officer Carson. An ambulance screamed down the dirt road to the place where everyone was standing around Willy. Next came the coroner's car. They all stood around, as if they were at some kind of reunion.

Lucky, Jim, and I were about thirty feet away. Mae walked over to see how we were. She looked old; she's never looked old before. I could see how upset she was. She looked at me and asked, "Scout, you OK?" Tears came to my eyes. I still couldn't talk. Every time I opened my mouth, the tears started again, and I couldn't say anything. I just nodded my head.

Lieutenant Glen walked over to me, put his arm around me, and said, "Scout, we have to talk."

Again, I just nod my head.

Mae looked at Lieutenant Glen and said, "Let's go back to the barn. It will be better there."

They put Willy's body in a black bag, and I knew this would be the last time I ever saw him. Lieutenant Glen told me to get in his car so he could drive me back to the barn. But as he headed for the car, I jumped on Lucky and just let him run. Jim somehow knew where we were going, so he took a shortcut.

Lieutenant Glen looked at Mae. "Where the hell is she going?"

"I don't know," Mae said, "but please let her go. She just needs a little space. She's been through a lot."

Lucky stopped at the big oak tree at the far end of the field. I dismounted, and Jim showed up. We sat under the tree, where it was quiet and no people were around.

Lieutenant Glen, upset, told Mae, "I need to talk to her right now." Mae replied as calmly as she could, "She'll be back. No one will be able to find her anyway."

Lieutenant Glen was getting very angry. "When will she be back? I need to talk to her *now*."

"Let her be with her friends. She'll be back soon," Mae told him.

"What friends? I don't need her talking to anyone but me." He was at the end of his rope.

"Her friends are Jim and Lucky, and if you push her too much, she'll surely run away. I just hope that those who shot that boy don't come after her."

"I'm worried about that the most," Lieutenant Glen said."

"Well," Jessie said as he walked up to help Mae get away from Lieutenant Glen, "I don't think anyone could find her right now, and if they did, that big old stud horse wouldn't let anyone near her." Jessie said as he walked up to help Mae get away from Lieutenant Glen. He saw that Mae was very upset over the whole ordeal.

"Well, the same gun that killed that boy could kill that horse." Lieutenant Glen wasn't letting up.

Jessie replied, "Take it easy, sir. She'll be back. Let's go back to the barn and talk about these missing horses. Scout will come back, and when she does, she'll

go to the barn. Gary should be at the farm by now, and he needs to know what's going on. He doesn't know anything yet, so let's talk to him, and by then Scout will be back."

Everyone loaded up in the cars. Jessie and Mae road with Lieutenant Glen, and Carson followed in his car. Back at the barn, there was a police car, and an officer was talking to Gary. Jessie knew this was going to be a long day and that Gary was going to be furious.

It was still morning, and Jessie thought to himself that it already felt like he has been up for days. But, mostly, all Jessie could think about was, Where did Scout go? Is she OK?

"I sure hope Scout comes back soon, Mae," Jessie said.

"I do too, Jessie. I do too." Mae was in tears.

* * *

For the next couple of hours, it was nothing but unanswered questions and Gary screaming on and on. "How did this happen?" Gary looked at Carson and said, "You knew there was horse stealing going on for about three months now, and you've done nothing about it. What are you going to do about my mares?" Carson said, "Right now, we not only have missing horses but a boy was killed. We're trying to get some answers, but Scout is the only one who saw anything, and we can't find her."

Gary was red-faced, eyes bugging out of his head, when he said, "What did Scout do—steal that stallion and leave? When she gets back, I want her off this farm for good."

Jessie stepped in. "She had nothing to do with any of this. So don't go blaming her, Gary."

"Well, where is she? Why isn't she here?"

"She's scared and upset. She'll be here soon." Then, he added quietly to himself, "I hope."

* * *

I sat under the tree with Jim and Lucky until the sky cleared and the sun came out. It would have been a pretty day—if only that dreadful picture of Willy being shot would have gotten out of my head.

What was he doing with those people? Why was he there? Would they have shot me if they had a chance?

I was scared—no question about that. I knew Jessie and Mae were worried about me; I shouldn't have run off like that. But I needed time to think about what had happened. I hoped they'd understand.

I eventually got on Lucky and headed back to the barn. We were in no hurry because I really did not want to talk about what had happened.

Chapter 3

WHERE DO WE GO NOW?

As we approached the barn, there must have been a dozen or more cars. I had Lucky stop before we got to the fence and got off of him. Gary did not like me messing around with Lucky. He said a stallion can never be trusted. And he is a horse trainer. How can you train horses and never trust them? I don't know, but Jessie said to keep him happy. Well, I couldn't just let Lucky go back in the pasture because the fence is down, so he had to go back to the barn with me. We would take whatever Gary dished out; it couldn't be as bad as what we have just gone through. Hopefully it would not be too bad.

Gary is a tall handsome man with dark brown eyes and dark tanned skin. Always wore a nice cowboy hat, tight jeans and pressed shirt. He works hard but never looked dirty. Sometimes he had the temper of a bobcat.

When we got close to the barn, Mae ran out and got Lucky, to put him up, while Jessie was distracting Gary from me. There were reporters and police everywhere. A reporter saw me first and started asking all kinds of questions. "Are you the girl they are looking for? Are you Scout? What happened? Where were you?"

Lieutenant Glen ran over, grabbed me, took me to his police car, and told me and Jim to get in. "Sit here till I get back, and don't talk to anyone." He wasn't happy at all. A few minutes later, he came back, got in the car, and without saying a word drove Jim and me away from the farm. I didn't know where we were going and didn't care.

Lieutenant Glen pulled into the police station and got out. He opened the door for me and Jim to get out, and we followed him inside. Everyone was looking at us—or maybe just at Jim. We went into an empty room. I sat down at the table, and Jim sat beside me. Lieutenant Glen left the room but soon came back with a drink and crackers for me and a bowl of water for Jim. I wasn't hungry, but the drink tasted good, and Jim looked like he was enjoying the water.

Lieutenant Glen asked me what happened? It took a few minutes, but I told him everything I knew, which wasn't much. "I went out looking for the missing horses and saw the fence down. I told Jim to go get Jessie. Then, as I started walking toward the fence that was down, I saw three figures. It was too foggy to tell who they were or even if they were men or women. One of the figures started running toward me and telling me to run away. When he got closer, I recognized him as Willy, the boy from my school. I heard a loud bang. Willy fell to the ground, and I ran. Jessie and Mae were coming across the pasture following Jim. Jim got to me first. When I turned around, the other two figures were gone, and Willy was lying on the ground, dead." I started crying again and couldn't stop.

Lieutenant Glen left the room again and came back with a roll of paper towels. He said with a smile on his face, "This is the best I can do. Do you think it is enough?"

I couldn't help but smile back. "I think it will be enough. Are you still mad at me?"

"No, just worried," he said.

"I'm sorry," I replied.

"It wasn't your fault. But I'm not sure what to do with you to keep you safe." He was getting back to himself.

"Can I go back to the farm, Lieutenant Glen?"

"No. How about staying with Sergeant Carson's family for a while?"

"I would rather stay with Jessie and Mae if that would be OK with you."

"I will talk to them and see." Lieutenant Glen was more relaxed, and I was calming down some also.

"What about school?" I asked.

"You need to stay out of sight for a while until I figure out what in the world is going on. But promise me if you see or remember anything you will call me."

"Yes, sir."

Lieutenant Glen called Jessie and Mae, and they came by and picked me up after feeding the horses that were left. When Jim and I got in the truck, Mae held me like a mama dog would hold a lost puppy that was just found. "You are OK now, my little friend." Mae stroked my hair, and I felt so safe, which was a nice feeling.

Jessie dropped of Mae, Jim, and me at their house and went back to the farm. Mae told me to go to the back room and lie down. I wasn't tired, but I did what I was told. Jim and I lay down on the bed and fell right to sleep.

＊＊＊

When I finally woke up, the smell of food was all through the house. I looked outside, and it was already dark. I didn't know how long I had been asleep, but it must have been awhile. Clean clothes were on the bed, and I couldn't wait to take a bath.

Mae walked in and brought me a towel and said, "Come on, bright eyes. Let's get clean before Jessie comes home, and we will eat dinner together. You are one dirty child. Jim came running in, all clean and smelling good. Then Mae said, "I already gave Jim his bath; now it's your turn. You'll feel better after you're clean and there's some food in your belly."

"How long was I asleep, Mae?"

"Long enough. Now, let's get going before Jessie gets here."

"OK, Mae."

I crawled out of bed and realized how stiff, dirty, and smelly I was. I walked into the bathroom, turned on the hot water, filled up the tub, and got in. It felt so good; I wanted to stay there the rest of my life. I put my head on the edge of the tub and fell right back to sleep. It was a short nap. I got out of the tub and dressed. I walked into the kitchen as Jessie came through the door.

Jessie and Mae's house was small. I had been there before. It had two bedrooms and one bathroom. Mae kept it very clean but warm and cozy. The table was already set, and dinner was ready to eat. I didn't know what happened to lunch, but by now I was hungry. The fried chicken, collards, and biscuits smelled so good.

Jessie walked in looking worn down. He looked so old for a young man. He always looked in charge, but now he was hunched over and walked slow. Jessie looked at the dinner table, then walked on through to the bathroom to wash up. He gave Mae a kiss on the cheek without saying a word. As he passed me, he patted me on the head, and he gave Jim a little pat also.

"It has been a long day for everyone," Mae said.

"Is Jessie OK, Mae?"

"Yes. He will be. This day has been hard on everyone."

Jessie walked in and sat down, and Mae brought him and me a plate of food. Jessie looked at it as if it were something he had never seen before.

"Jessie, has something else happened?" Mae was worried too.

"No, dear. No one knows who that boy was. The school had no information on him. It looks like he just went to school, and everyone just took it for granted that he belonged there. We don't even know if Willy was his real name. It is just sad that the poor boy had nothing going for him and had to go so violently."

Mae noticed that I was tearing up again and was just looking at my food. "Jessie, dear. Can we talk about this after eating? You and Scout have not had anything all day." She turned her sights on me.

"Sorry, dear. Scout, eat your food. Mae worked hard so we could have something to eat. I'm just glad that you have people looking after you who care and that you did not end up with no one."

"Me too, Jessie, I love you both very much, and thank you for everything you do for me and Jim. How was Lucky when you left? Is he OK?"

"He is OK. Now eat your dinner."

The rest of the meal was eaten in silence. After eating, Mae gave Jim a plate of food, which he liked very much. The day didn't seem to bother *his* appetite.

Mae and I cleaned up the dishes and had just sat down to watch television when Jessie said, "Scout, go take Jim for a walk, I need to talk to Mae for a minute."

"OK, Jessie. Come on, Jim. Let's go check things out." As I walked out the door, I could tell Jessie wasn't happy about something that concerned me. I didn't feel like going for a walk, but Jim needed to go out. We walked around, looking at the neighborhood where Jessie and Mae lived. It seemed to be a nice place, but it was hard to tell at night. I was really tired, and all I wanted to do was go back to bed.

Willy was still in my head, and I couldn't get rid of him. "Run," he was saying. "Run"–over and over again. Maybe in the morning things would be better.

As we were walking along, mainly in circles a car drove up. My heart started beating, and Jim was growling. It stopped right in front of us, and we didn't know what to do. The lights on the car were very bright, and we couldn't see a thing. Jim and I turned to run away when someone called out our names. "Scout! You and Jim stop. It's me, Bobby Carson. I was just checking on you."

"Oh, hi Sergeant Carson. Didn't recognize you when you pulled up."

"You know you can call me Bobby. What's going on? You OK?"

"Yes. Jim and I are just going for a walk. Jessie wanted to talk to Mae alone."

"So they sent you outside?"

"Yes. Jim needed to go to the bathroom. We're not going very far."

"I don't think they realized the seriousness of this situation. You need to go inside now, please."

"OK, OK. But what's going on? Why are all these things happening?"

"We'll talk about it later. But for right now, humor me and go back in the house."

"Are you coming to talk to Jessie?"

"Yes, I am. Now, let's go in the house."

Bobby, Jim, and I walked in the house together. Jessie seemed startled at the sight of Bobby.

"How's it going?" Bobby asked Jessie.

"OK, I guess. What can we do for you? Do you have any new information on what happened today?" Jessie didn't look like he liked the idea of Bobby being there.

"No new information. Just checking to see if everything was all right here. *Is* everything all right here?" Bobby asked with a strange tone in his voice.

"Yes, everything is fine." You could tell Jessie wasn't happy about this surprise visit.

"Can I get you something to eat, Sergeant Carson?" Mae said, trying to break the tension. "We have some leftovers, and they're still warm. Would you like some?"

"I'd like a cup of coffee…if that would be all right?"

"Sure. Coming right up. Jessie, would you like some?"

"Yes, thank you, Mae."

"Come on, Scout. You can help me in the kitchen." Mae was trying her best to not let things get out of control. Mae made the coffee, and I took it out to Jessie and Bobby. They were talking, but I could tell it wasn't a real friendly conversation. So I delivered the coffee and went to my room with Jim.

Soon after, Bobby left. I didn't care what he wanted; I just wanted to go back to sleep and hope that none of this ever happened. I got into the bed, and Jim got on the bed beside me. And before I could turn over, I was asleep. The next day would be another day, and it had to be better than this one.

In my sleep all I could do was dream about Willy. He was sitting there, looking at me. At least he wasn't yelling at me to run. He looked peaceful and in no pain. I liked looking at him. He was a very handsome young man. I could see every detail of his face, and it made me feel better. He touched me on the shoulder and said he would miss me also. Right then, I woke up and jumped clean out of bed. Jim didn't know what happened and jump down to stand right next to me. I didn't know whether to be sad or glad that I got to see Willy again. It was eight o'clock in the morning. I had never slept this long in my life. I hoped today would be better.

I got up; took another long, hot shower; and got dressed. Jim and I walked into the kitchen, where Mae was. She was fixing me breakfast. "Has Jessie already gone, Mae?"

"Oh yes, dear. He left hours ago."

"Can I go to the farm later, Mae?"

"No, dear. You and I are going to stay here today and clean up this house. It's time for spring cleaning."

"OK, Mae. I'll help do anything you want."

"First, eat your breakfast and take Jim out to go to the bathroom. And then we'll talk about what I have planned for the day. OK?"

"OK."

Mae put a plate of pancakes and bacon in front of me, and it smelled so good, but my belly felt like it had a big rock in it. I tried to eat, but there was no room in my belly.

"Are you all right, Scout? Please eat something."

"I'm OK. But I just can't eat. Can I tell you something, Mae? And will you not think I'm crazy?"

"Sure, Scout. Tell me whatever you want. After yesterday, I would never think you were crazy. You are the bravest person I've ever met."

I told Mae about my dream. She hung on every word, as if I were giving some kind of important speech. When I was done, I asked her, "Am I crazy, Mae?"

"No, dear. And I think it's good Willy came to see you. Were you scared when you saw him?"

"No."

"Good. We'll talk about this as we clean the house. I think the spirit world is a blessing. So don't be scared of Willy. Let him be there for you."

"Thank you, Mae. I knew you'd understand." I took another bite of pancake, and it went down a little easier. Mae always knew how to make things better.

After eating I took Jim out, and he did his business right away. He didn't waste any time. Poor guy. He really had to go.

The neighborhood was very quiet. I guess everyone was either at work or school. Jim and I were just looking around when a voice in my head said, "Go in the house, Scout." I didn't think twice about it; I just went in the house.

When I was inside, Mae said, "Girl, you look like you saw a ghost. What's wrong?"

"I didn't see anyone, but I sure *heard* someone." Suddenly, there was a knock on the door.

"Scout, go into the kitchen and stay out of sight till I see who this is." I did as I was told. Jim and I went into the kitchen.

Mae said, "Who is it?"

The man at the door said, "I need to talk to you about the little girl you are letting stay here."

Mae opened the door. "Who are you?" she said with confidence.

"I have come to pick up the girl," he said.

"I'm sorry. Sergeant Carson came by last night and picked her up and took her to the police station. I believe that is where they went." Mae was good.

"I was told she was here. And I see fresh dog poop. She does have a dog, right?"

"Yes, she does. And Jim is staying here with us for right now. What do you want with the girl?" "I'm here from social services; her parents want her home."

"Well, you will have to go talk to the police because I don't know where they took her." Mae was very convincing. Jim came into the room, and Mae told the man he was her dog. Jim was growling at the man, and Mae said, "Do you want Jim also?"

"No," the man said.

"May I have your name please, sir, so I can tell the police that you were here—so they can straighten this out with you and her parents?"

"That will be OK. I will go talk to the police myself. But I hope you aren't telling me a lie—because if I find out that she is here, you, madame, will be in big trouble, trouble you don't want."

"Well, I have a lot of work to do, so please excuse me," Mae said as she closed the door in his face.

The man walked around the house to the back door at the kitchen. I was standing in the corner, where he couldn't see me but I could see him. He was a tall man with dark hair. He hadn't shaved his face in a while. He didn't look like he had had much sleep either. He was too scruffy to be working for the social services office.

Mae came into the kitchen—with a shotgun—and headed straight for the door. I'd never seen Mae with a gun—didn't know they even had one. I'd never seen Mae look so mean. She's a very pretty lady but not at this moment. The man at the door turned and ran off, like a rabbit that just saw a pack of dogs coming.

"Mae, what are you going to do with that gun?" I asked, scared to death.

"That man had to go. There was something about him I didn't like at all."

"Well, I believe he got the message," I told Mae. She looked at me and smiled, and the sweet Mae that I knew was back. She put the gun down, and we both looked at each other and started laughing. "I didn't know you knew how to use a gun."

"I don't!" We both laughed even harder. It felt good to laugh some. It had been a long time, and we needed a break.

Mae called Jessie and told him what had happened. Jessie was home almost before Mae hung up the phone. With him was Lieutenant Glen and Bobby.

"What are we going to do with you, my little friend?" Lieutenant Glen was looking at me with that nice smile of his.

"I don't know," I said. "I'm so sorry for all the trouble I've caused everyone."

"Mae, I can't believe you got that gun. What on earth were you going to do with it?" Jessie said to Mae.

"I was going to shoot that scraggly fool at the door," she answered back with determination in her voice.

"You've never even shot the gun before—and, not only that, it wasn't loaded."

"Then I guess I would've *beaten* that man to death with it."

"All I got to say to that is you better stay on Mae's good side from now on," Lieutenant Glen said. He was holding back a laugh, but he was grinning from ear to ear.

"What are we going to do about this, Lieutenant Glen?" Jessie said. "We can't live like this: my wife carrying a gun, some strange man coming to kidnap a child. What are we going to do? Do you have any idea who is behind all this?"

"No. I'm not sure what all this is about, but I have some ideas—just not enough evidence to bring forward at this time." Lieutenant Glen was back in his business mode again. "I do agree that we need to do something with Scout. We need to find a safe place for her. Does anyone have any thoughts? Bobby, would you and Mae take Scout in the other room? I want to talk to Jessie alone for a moment please."

"Jessie, what are your thoughts on the situation? Do you have any idea what is going on or any thoughts on where Scout can stay? I can tell you aren't happy with this setup, and I'm not either. I was really hoping they wouldn't come looking for her, but now that they have…I believe that was what that man was after. What do you think we should do?"

"Did anyone call the social services office to see if they sent someone out here?" Jessie asked, hoping maybe they did.

"Yes. I checked, and no one from there was sent out here. Her parents are out of town and can't be reached. I don't know when they will even be back; they never cared about that child, anyway. It's a shame; she's a good kid."

"Well it's going to break Mae's heart, and mine too, but she can't stay here. I love that child, but she isn't safe here. What are we going to do? And after she's gone, will *we* be safe, in our own home?"

"I'll have a patrol car come out and check around here on a regular basis. In the meantime, help me find a safe place for Scout. Can she stay just a little longer? I understand this is dangerous for you and Mae, so, if not, I'll take her with me now. Just tell me what you want to do."

"Yes, she can stay a little longer. Mae loves that child, and I do too. I don't want any harm to come to her or anybody else."

"Thank you, Jessie. I'll have people keep an eye on your place, and I'll be checking in also. Here is my cell phone number," he said handing Jessie his card. "If you need anything, just call me direct. We'll get through this. I promise."

"Thank you, Lieutenant Glen. I just hope things get better. It's not even lunchtime, and all this has already messed up my day. I'm so worried about my wife and Scout—not to mention that poor boy from yesterday. Have you found out anything about him?"

Lieutenant Glen was looking a little worn out but said, "No. Haven't found anything out about him yet. It's just a shame: people have children and don't want to look after them. I don't understand how they can do that. I think he's just another lost child, like Scout. If Scout vanished today, I don't think her parents would even put a missing-child bulletin out on her. I think that's the same situation we have with this young man—who we now know only as *Willy*."

"You're a good man, Lieutenant Glen. Mae and I will do the best we can."

"Thank you, Jessie. We need to get back out there, so call me if you need anything. Bobby, come on. We need to go." Bobby came back into the room, then he and Lieutenant Glen walked out the door, got into two separate cars, and drove away.

Mae looked at Jessie and said, "What are they going to do, Jessie?"

"I don't know. But do you two think you can stay out of trouble for a little while so I can go back to work?"

"Yes. Sure, Jessie. Just load that gun, and we'll fight off the demons."

"You aren't helping me any, Mae."

"Just kidding, Jessie. Go to work."

＊

When Jessie returned to the farm, Gary was talking to the owners, Mr. and Mrs. Hunter. They didn't look happy, but they did look genuinely upset. Gary asked Jessie to come and help explain the details of what had happened the day before. Mr. Hunter asked Gary to give them a list of the missing horses. They were going to meet with the police in the afternoon to discuss what to do next.

Mr. Hunter asked Jessie, "Where is the girl?"

Jessie looked at Gary, who shook his head then looked toward Jessie. Jessie told Mr. Hunter, "I think the police have her. I'm not sure."

"How can you not be sure? That little girl follows you around like a dog on a leash. Where is the girl? I will ask just one more time." Mr. Hunter went from upset to downright mad.

Jessie wasn't sure what to do, so he said, "I'm sorry, but I'm not sure. You need to talk to Lieutenant Glen."

"Well, that is exactly what I intend to do. That child is not allowed on this property anymore. I'm not going to be blamed for a lost child. That is just what I need.

Gary, the people we lease Lucky and Maple from will be here this afternoon to pick them up. They're worried they will be stolen also. I told them I didn't think the thieves would be back—with all the things that have happened—but they want the horses home anyway, so get them ready."

"OK, Mr. Hunter. I'll take care of it."

"Jessie, we need to talk later, but right now I need to get to the police station." Mr. and Mrs. Hunter got in their car and left.

"Jessie, you need to go call Lieutenant Glen and let him know what you told the Hunters about Scout."

"Why? Did you not want me to tell them where she was, Gary?"

"Before you got here, they just seemed way too interested in Scout for my comfort. I've never seen them act like this before. I may be wrong, but I don't like it–something's not right."

"OK, I'll call Lieutenant Glen so he'll know what I've told them. He gave me his cell number so I could call him directly."

Jessie went to call Lieutenant Glen, and Gary went to get Lucky and Maple ready to go back to their home. When Jessie came back to help Gary, Gary said, "Jessie, what happened at your house today?"

"Some stranger came by wanting Scout. He pretended to be with social services. We really need to find a safe place for Scout. Mae and I can't live like this. If something ever happened to Mae or that child, I couldn't forgive myself."

"Jessie, I have an idea…if you want to hear it?"

"Yes, please. Anything."

"The people who will be picking up Lucky are friends of mine. They aren't real fond of the Hunters, but since I'm working here, they let them lease Lucky to breed some of the mares. Anyway, I could ask them to let Scout stay with them for a while, till things calm down around here. They have four children of their own–but wouldn't mind one more–I don't think. I could ask them."

"Lieutenant Glen did say we need to find somewhere she can be safe," Jessie replied.

"What did Lieutenant Glen say about the Hunters?"

"He said he would handle them and 'Thanks for the heads-up.' Do you really think these people will let Scout stay with them? How well do you know them? Where do they live? How far away will she be, and is it far enough away? I'm so scared for that girl; I'm about to go out of my mind.

"They live on an island off the coast of South Carolina, on a plantation. This is the best family I've ever known. If they do agree to take her, she'll be in a good place. Should I give them a call?"

"Gary, why are you doing this? You never acted like you liked Scout."

"I've never *disliked* her. I just didn't think living in a barn was a good place for a young girl. I was always afraid she'd get hurt, and I didn't want that. I'm sorry if you thought I was too hard on her, but after yesterday I can see she's a strong girl, and I'd like to help her if I can. It's clear her parents want nothing to do with her. I tried to reach them yesterday, and one of her brothers said the parents are gone for a month—and if she comes back there, they will beat her up again. Why would they say that?"

"They used to beat her up all the time. That's why she's here. Well, call your friends, and see what they say. But we can't tell anyone else about this. I'll call Lieutenant Glen after we hear if the people you know will let her stay there."

Gary said, "I'll go call them and see. They should be here this afternoon for the horses. How do you think Scout will feel about this?"

"She doesn't have many options." Jessie looked worried. "Let's just keep this between us, if you don't mind, Gary."

"OK, that's fine. No problem here."

* * *

Later that day, Gary walked up to Jessie. "I called the Blakes, and they said they'd be happy to let her stay a little while, plus they could use the help. I told them how well she gets along with horses, dogs, and all kinds of critters."

"What time will they be here?"

"They should be here around five, and the Hunters have gone to a polo match and won't be back till around seven. So I think this will work well for Scout."

36

"It's three now, so I'll go get her and have her back here at five. I hope we're doing the right thing, Gary."

"Don't worry. Mr and Mrs. Blake are good people, and they have four sons who are just as good as they can be. They've never been in any trouble and make straight As in school. I think they will be good for her, and maybe she can go back to school."

"OK then. That is what we will do. I'll see you shortly with Scout." Jessie walked to his truck. "I worry so about this girl. I hope I'm doing the right thing," he said to himself.

Five o'clock came around faster than anyone could've imagined, but there I stood, looking at the truck and trailer that was going to take me, Maple, and Lucky–to somewhere I'd never even heard of. Gary was standing next to and holding Lucky. Lucky looked happy he was leaving, and that was comforting.

A tall, young man came walking out from the back of the trailer. He had on blue jeans, boots, a nice shirt, and a straw cowboy hat. I couldn't even see his face. That hat was so big that I thought he could curl up and sleep in it. This made me smile. I looked up at Jessie, who had tears rolling down his cheeks. I said, "It's going to be OK, Jessie. I can feel it; I know it. Trust me on this one."

"I hope so, my little friend. But if things aren't right, you call me, and I'll come get you, you hear me?"

"Yes, Jessie, I hear you, and I promise I'll call you. Who else do I have?"

With that, I picked up my little bag of clothes and food, which Mae had made for me, and Jim and I headed for the truck. Gary and the boy with the big hat loaded Lucky and Maple in the trailer. I put Jim in the back of the truck, and then I entered on the passenger side. The boy with the big hat bounced in the driver side and pulled his big hat off, with the biggest grin on his face. He had a brown complexion and big, brown eyes and–

"Hi! My name's Tommy," he said, on his third attempt.

With nothing else to say, I replied, "Hi. My name's Scout."

"Let's bring your friend up front with us. I think that would be a lot safer, plus he'll get lonely back there. It's going to be a long drive."

Tommy kept looking at me. Realizing that he was waiting for me, I jumped out and got Jim and brought him into the truck. Jim looked relieved; he never really liked riding in the back. When everyone was settled, Tommy started the truck, and we pulled away. I looked back at Jessie and waved goodbye. Jessie watched the truck go until he couldn't see it anymore. He got in his truck and drove back home to Mae.

"Where are we going, Tommy?"

"It's going to be a long drive; it took four hours getting here. I think you'll like it. My mom and dad work for a big plantation on an island off the coast of South Carolina. There's no place like it in the world."

"Island? I've never even seen the ocean. Will the island sink? Well, isn't it surrounded by water? How do we get there? By boat?"

"You ask too many questions, Little Sister. But we have a long drive, and I'll try to tell you everything you want to know."

"Why did you call me Little Sister? I'm not your sister."

"My grandma says that we're all related, and when people figure that out and realize we are all family, maybe people would stop hurting each other. You will meet Grandma; she lives with us also."

"Do you think they'll like me? You don't know me. Your family don't know me. What if no one likes me? What will I do?" I started to panic. Jim jumped up and licked me on the face, wagging his tail, like he was trying to tell me it would be OK. Tommy just looked at me and winked, then smiled. I sat back and looked out the window. It was going to be a nice day.

It wasn't long before the sun was going down. The sky was bright orange; that made me feel good all over. I don't know why, but everything was calm. Tommy was listening to music that was a little country and folk mixed. This was the most relaxed that I'd been in a long time. Jim even looked relaxed.

Tommy said without looking, "Are you getting hungry, Scout?"

"A little. Mae packed us some sandwiches if you want one."

"No. I have to get gas, and we'll get something there. I know a pretty good place to eat."

"But I don't have any money."

"No worries, Little Sister. We are family. It's OK. I'll pay for you."

"Are you sure?"

"You're fine. Just sit back and enjoy the ride."

I sat back with my head against the window, watching the trees go by, thinking of Willy and then trying *not* to think about him. What if none of this had happened? Would he have liked me? And would I have liked him? Why did this happen, and would it ever be OK again? And what is "OK"? Questions. All I had were questions, but my head had no answers. I felt like a big question mark...Willy came walking toward me with Jim by his side. He looked straight at me. "Jim said we needed to talk."

I almost jumped out the window. I had no idea where I was.

Tommy grabbed me and said, "Whoa, girl! Where're you going? You OK? You fell asleep, and the next thing you did was try to jump out of the truck." Confused and trying to get my senses back, I remembered where I was. Looking at Tommy, I told him I was fine. He didn't believe me but let it go. He turned the blinker on and pulled into a small truck stop with a restaurant next to it. He got out and walked around the truck and opened the door for me. I didn't know what to do.

Tommy smiled and said, "Get out, and let's get something to eat. Then we'll get gas."

I got out of the truck and walked slowly to the restaurant.

"You OK, Scout?"

"I think so."

"You don't sound so sure."

I was still thinking about Willy. I felt like I was sleepwalking. I looked at Tommy and just said, "I'm not sure."

Tommy ordered us both a cheeseburger and fries, and all I could do was stare at it.

"Sorry, Tommy. I'm not hungry."

"Well, Jim is going to love me because guess what he's getting for dinner."

"Yes, he'll like that, for sure. Sorry, Tommy. It just has been a long day."

"It's OK, Little Sister. I'm here for you, and when you need me to, I'll listen. You have nothing to feel sorry for."

"Thank you, Big Brother." I looked up at Tommy. With a big grin on his face, he said, "I could get used to that." He made me smile as we walked back to the truck. He pulled the truck around to the gas pumps and filled up. Then we were on our way.

As Jim was finishing his cheeseburger, I asked Tommy, "How long was I asleep?"

"About an hour, I guess. You were out of it—I mean, sound asleep. Did you have a bad dream?"

I wished Mae were here to talk to. "I don't know. I mean, kind of. But it's hard to talk about, and I'm not sure I can talk about it." I didn't know what I was allowed to discuss. For the moment, I was quiet.

"It's OK. No problem." Tommy kept his eyes on the road, and we traveled in silence for a while. Every now and then, Tommy would look in my direction and wonder what on earth happened to me.

But now wasn't the time to ask questions. The moon was starting to come up, and it was a big full moon. Tommy put a CD in the player, and it was someone talking about a full moon and how it made all the little critters a little jumpy. I asked Tommy, "Who is that?"

"Jerry Jeff Walker, one of my favorites. He always makes me happy." So we listened to the CD, and he was right; it *was* fun. Tommy would sing along, smile, and every now and then look over to check on me. He made me feel safe.

It wasn't long before Tommy said, "Here we go—crossing the bridge."

"What bridge?"

"The bridge that goes over to the island."

The moon was very bright, and I could see the reflection of the moon on the water. It looked just like it did in the sky. I found that fascinating—the stars, moon, and...something else in the water.

"Tommy, what's that in the water? Is it a shark or something?"

"Little Sister, that's a dolphin! He won't hurt you. Little Sister, you're going to be so much fun. You'll love it here! Just wait and see. You'll have so much fun and a lot to see. I can't wait to show you."

Chapter 4

THE ISLAND

As we drove over the bridge, we entered a new world. It was flat, and water was everywhere. You could see it glimmer in the moonlight. There were these huge trees on the side of the road, and they had something hanging off them. They looked like ghosts hanging from the trees. I wasn't sure what to think. Would I ever see anyone I had known again? Would I ever see Jessie and Mae again? What about the horses? Would they miss me?

Tommy looked over at me. "You OK, my friend?"

"I don't know. All this has happened so fast. I have so many questions and no answers. I feel like I'm drowning, but I'm not in water. I didn't think about how I'd feel leaving everything and everyone I know. I feel so lost, like no one cares. I feel like a small rock that just fell off the biggest mountain of all, and no one even knew I was gone." I just let it fly. I was so tired of going along with whatever anyone told me to do. "Sorry you asked?"

Tommy gave me a look of real understanding and concern. It wasn't what I was expecting. I felt foolish for what I had said.

Tommy calmly said, "Just you wait. You're going to love it here. Things are different here. People are different here. Just you wait.

People don't make you whole. You wait. Once you find yourself, you're going to be a brand-new Scout."

What in the world is he talking about? I asked myself. A new Scout? What's that about? Another question—that's just what I need.

After a short while, we turned down a long driveway. Huge trees lined the driveway. They all had ghosts hanging from them. I wondered if they would be there when the sun came in the morning. The moon was big and bright. I don't think I've ever seen the moon so big. I was so tired. I just wanted to go to sleep in a bed, and maybe this would all be a bad dream.

I knew Jim needed to go out and pee, and so did I.

But I was too embarrassed to tell Tommy, so I hoped we would be wherever we were going soon. I could see some lights up ahead, which was a relief.

Lucky could tell he was home. He was stomping the floor of the trailer and whining at the top of his lungs. Maple was just as quiet as always. I was glad they were with us.

We finally stopped in front of a super-nice big barn. A young boy walked out of the barn, with a big cowboy hat on like Tommy's, and he walked to the of the trailer and started unloading the horses. What is it with these big hats? Just another question. "Scout, stop it," I said to myself.

Tommy looked at me and said, "That's John. He's my younger brother." As we got out of the truck, Jim ran off to go to the bathroom, and Tommy told me there was a bathroom in the barn. I guess he figured I needed one, and he was right. I ran into the barn to find it.

When I came out of the barn, Tommy and John had already unloaded the horses. Tommy had my bags of clothes and sandwiches, which I had forgotten about, but now I was hungry. We headed to the house. I couldn't see it clearly due to all the trees around it. The moon was so bright, casting shadows all around the house.

We walked into the house through the kitchen and sat down at the table. I was looking at the bag with the sandwiches in it when Tommy said, "Girl, you must be hungry by now."

"Can I have my sandwiches now? I *am* rather hungry."

"Don't you want me to fix you something to eat?" Tommy looked at the brown paper sack.

"No, I want what Mae fixed me. If that's OK?"

"Sure, have at it."

John looked at Tommy and said, "You could fix *me* something if you like, Tommy."

"Yeah right. Go fix your own, brother. Have Mom and Dad got back yet, John?"

"No. Frankie called earlier and said they would be back tomorrow. They said if we needed anything, call Grandma."

"Who's Frankie?" I asked, eating my sandwich and letting Jim have a bite or two.

"Frankie is our other brother, along with Mike. They are with Mom and Dad." Tommy looked at Jim and said, "Can I give Jim some dog food?"

"Yes, please," I answered for him. "I didn't have any to bring." I looked around for other dogs but didn't see any. "Do you have dogs here?"

John laughed. "Oh yes. They're in the bed in my room. They can be pretty lazy this time of night."

"I'm pretty tired also. Is there a place I can lie down?"

They showed me a room with a big bed in it, and Tommy looked at me and said, "There you go, Little Sister. Have good dreams. And Jim can sleep on the bed with you if you like." They showed me where the bathroom was, so I brushed my teeth and crawled into bed. Jim got up next to me. The bed was so comfortable, and that was my last memory of that night.

＊＊＊

Early the next morning, Jim woke me up. I was in such a deep sleep that when I opened my eyes, I had no idea where I was. The room was big. The bed was big. The bed was nice.

But after a few minutes, I realized where I was. "OK, Jim. I'm up. Let's go find outside." Not sure how we got into the house last night, we wandered down a hallway and found a door that went outside. It was a big, wooden door, with no markings, thick and heavy. It wasn't locked, so I opened it to look out.

Jim bolted out the door in a flash. He really needed to go. "Bless his heart." That is what Mae would say. I miss them so much. I walked out onto the porch, and it was a big porch. It had flowers and plants of all kinds. It smelled like a spring day, but I knew it was fall.

The air outside had a little chill to it but not much, but the air itself had a strange smell to it. I never smelled anything like that before. There was a bench swing over to the right, so I walked over and sat in it, and at the edge of the yard were three deer, grazing on the green grass. In the tree next to them was a bald eagle. I had never seen a bald eagle in person before, but I had seen pictures of them. It's hard not to know with that big, white head.

Then I heard an owl hoot...and hoot again. I found him by the water. There was a big river of water. As I was looking at it, I saw a huge something come up out of the water. It looked like fire. It was just a tip coming out of the water. A lady walked out of the house and sat down next to me. She wasn't a big lady but not a dainty one either. She sat down and put her arm around my shoulder. By this time, the big fireball was about halfway up.

"Is that the sun?" I had to ask. I had never seen the sun come up like this before.

"Yes, that's the sun," the lady said to me. Suddenly, with a whoosh, some spray came up out of the water, then there was a hump with a fin.

"What's that? I saw something like it when we crossed over the bridge last night."

"Those are dolphins. They're feeding in the creek this morning."

"Creek? Are you kidding me? The creeks where I come from have tadpoles. This creek has monsters?"

The lady laughed. A man walked out of the house. The sun was up pretty good now, and he sat down on the other side of me.

"Are you the Blakes?"

"Yes, we are."

"Child, you're going to love it here. It's going to be nice having a little girl. I've been feeling a little outnumbered around here," Mrs. Blake said.

Jim ran up on the porch, wagging his tail, jumping up and down as happy as he could be.

"One thing's for sure: Jim's happy," I said. He put a smile on my face. I sat back and watched the dolphins swim in huge creek.

I woke up to the smell of bacon, and it smelled good. I was in the bed. I looked over to the side of the bed, and there were five dogs looking at me. Jim was first and then a collie, lab, shepherd, and another border collie that looked like Jim. They all had their heads on the bed.

Then I realized where I was, back in the bed. How did I get here? Was everything a dream? Did I not see the sun come up? Tommy looked in on me and said, "Come get something to eat."

"OK," I said reluctantly.

I followed Tommy into the kitchen, where there were a lot of people. I recognized John and Tommy, but the other two young boys I didn't know. All the boys got up, grabbed book bags, and headed to the door. They all looked at me and said, "Bye, Little Sister. See you later"—except for the youngest, who walked over and asked, "How old are you?"

I told him, "Thirteen."

"Man! I will still be 'Baby Boy.' OK then," he said, giving me a kiss on the cheek. "Bye, Big Sister. See you this afternoon."

There were three other older men who, I guessed, worked there.

The lady cooking was the same lady in my dreams, and so was the man at the end of the table. I said, "Good morning, everyone," still blushing from the little boy kissing me on the cheek.

"Good morning, dear," the lady said from the stove.

"Good morning," everyone else said at one time.

"Morning," I said, feeling a little out of place. Then a plate of food was put down in front of me. I felt better after eating.

After eating, the older man looked at me and said, "You ready to go to the barn?

I hear you are quite the hand around horses.

Is that true, my little friend?" He was looking at me as if he knew me all my life.

"I do OK. Who told you about me?"

"You are quite the conversation around here lately."

"I know, and I don't like it either."

"It'll be over soon. Let's go see how the horses are after their late-night trip."

Chapter 5

THE INVESTIGATION

Lieutenant Glen was sitting at his desk looking at paperwork that he didn't want to deal with. How could two young children get so involved in this mess? he thought. He heard the office door close. "Bobby, is that you?"

"Yes, I'll be in there in just a minute."

Bobby walked over to his desk to check messages. No messages. That was odd. But, OK, it had been a long day. He walked into Lieutenant Glen's office. "What's up, Lieutenant?" Bobby sat down in front of the lieutenant's desk.

"Bobby, look at all this paperwork on this horse-stealing case. Do we know any more than we did a week ago? Everyone is getting down on me. I mean, really—a child was killed. No one even knows who this child was. He was maybe twelve years old, for Christ's sake. He was just a boy. I feel for this boy's parents. Do you think the boy was kidnapped? We don't even know the boy's name. Another twelve-year-old said his name is Willy…said she met him at school. No one at the school even knows who she is talking about, except two more twelve-year-olds who said he and Scout would eat lunch with them. The school has no record of this boy at all. So can you please, Sergeant

Carson, give me something on this case? I thought the Old West was over. Now I'm dealing with horse stealing. I don't even like horses. Or if I did, I don't any longer. So please give me something."

"I got nothing," Bobby said, a little confused. He didn't usually get called "Sergeant Carson." He went on: "I did check all the local barns and empty pastures I could find—and, so far, nothing. I called the surrounding counties to be on the lookout for anything that might be our people. I've had my guys check any and all horse trailers. People are getting pretty pissed off. You will maybe get some calls on that. I mean, I'm like you. Those horses didn't just fall off the face of the earth. And that boy wasn't plucked from the stars."

"Sorry, Bobby. I'm just at my wit's end. I'm going to call in some extra people. Do you know Vic Orr?" Bobby nodded his head. "Well, I've been thinking about calling him in for a different perspective. What do you think? I know this is your case, but I need something to happen soon. And maybe he can see something we're missing."

"OK. I'm game because I got nothing."

"Be here in the morning at eight, and I'll set up a meeting."

"OK. I'll see you in the morning." Bobby got up, and you could tell he was tired. He walked by the clock and looked, then checked his watch. He did this every time he left the office. Lieutenant Glen got up from his desk, turned the light out, closed the door, and locked it. He also had had a long day.

The next morning Bobby walked into his office early. He wanted to check all of his notes that he had on the case. He didn't want this Vic Orr person to catch him off guard. He had heard Vic's name before but had never met him. What he did know was that Vic Orr was a long-time friend of Lieutenant Glen.

"You OK, Bobby?" The voice startled Bobby. He turned and saw Lieutenant Glen. "What's wrong, Bobby? Did you not hear me when I walked in? I didn't mean to startle you."

"It's OK. I just wanted to be ready when your friend gets here. I was going over all of my notes so I could answer as many questions as I could."

"This isn't a test, Bobby. I just wanted someone outside the box to look at this. Maybe he can see something we're missing. Sometimes I think we're too close to this case. Can we just see what he has to say, with open minds?"

"Yes. Sorry. I'm OK with this, really. I don't mean to be so out of sorts. I agree with what you're thinking, and I'm OK."

"Thanks, Bobby. Now, let's get this dog-and-pony show on the road."

Bobby smiled at him and said, "And you told me you weren't a cowboy. Sure sound like one to me."

The office door opened, and in walked a tall man with big, blue eyes. Men normally don't notice such, but they looked as though they scanned the room when he walked in. He walked right past Bobby and headed straight for Lieutenant Glen, who was heading toward his office. The tall man walked up behind Lieutenant Glen and touched his shoulder. "Hello, Adam." Lieutenant Glen jumped and then realized who it was.

"Vic, you scared the mess out of me. How are you doing? How are your mom and dad?"

"Good. Everyone is good."

"Well, come on in and sit down. Bobby, could you join us please?"

"Yes, on my way." Bobby looked confused. This guy didn't look like he could drive a car, much less help on this case. Bobby grabbed some of his things and took them with him. As he walked into the office, he noticed that the furniture had been moved around. Lieutenant Glen's desk was moved to the middle of the room, and the two chairs that normally sat in front of his desk were now on either end. Vic was sitting in the chair the furthest from the door. Lieutenant Glen said to Bobby, "Please, sit here." He pointed to the chair closer to the door, as far away from Vic as he could get him. Lieutenant Glen's desk sat between them, like a wall.

"What's going on?" Bobby asked. He was getting frustrated with all this." Just sit down. I'll explain. Vic here is autistic, which is why I have this set up like this. He doesn't like to be too close to anyone.

But he also sees things in a different light. I've known him all of his life. He has also helped me on other cases. So I asked him to come look at this one. So please, Bobby, give him a chance."

Bobby looked at this young man sitting in the chair on the other side of the room. He was very clean, with a blue button-down shirt, khaki pants, and what looked like a brand-new pair of tennis shoes. He sat looking at the ceiling like he was fixating on something.

Bobby said, "What do you want me to do? I don't understand."

"Vic," Lieutenant Glen continued. "Vic, you read the report. What do you think about the case? Do you think that the horses are still here? Are they gone?"

Vic didn't look down but answered, "The horses are still around. The bad men are still here also. There is going to be an accident. Four men will be driving two trucks. Three will die. The fourth will be able to answer your questions."

"When Vic? When will this happen?" Lieutenant Glen asked.

"Don't know. But it will be wet. That is all I know." That was the first time Vic looked down from the ceiling. A lady walked into the office. "Adam, are you done with my son? We have to go pick up Mary Beth from school. You know she can be a real pickle when things don't go her way."

Vic perked up and said, "Yeah, a real sour pickle." Vic had a little smirk on his face, like he knew that was funny but didn't know what to do about it.

Lieutenant Glen laughed and looked at Vic and said, "That's a good one.

Nancy, thanks for letting us speak with him."

Nancy and Vic were leaving when she turned around and said, "I'd do anything for my big brother. See ya later."

Vic turned around and looked at Bobby and said, "That man has a secret, Adam. Bye."

"What the hell was that supposed to mean? And what was all that about? That was the craziest thing I've ever seen. I don't have any secrets on this case. Am I now a suspect?"

"No, not at all. Calm down. Let me explain. Vic is a savant, which means he can know things. No one knows why or how; he just does. He just knows things sometimes, and other times he knows nothing."

"What about him saying I have a secret? I don't have any secrets."

"We all have secrets. It didn't mean anything about the case. He's done that to all of us...which has started a lot of foolish arguments. You're OK. Now, can we talk about the case?"

"Yes. But explain to me what in the world that boy talking about. I've never felt so confused."

"Well, according to Vic, these guys are still here, and the horses are still here also. I don't know how he knows things, but he hasn't been wrong yet. He also said there was going to be an accident. Vic said it would be wet. That could be driving through water, rain, or just a wet road. You take what makes sense to you and run with it."

"When do we get to the part where something makes sense," Bobby said, still looking like he was at a magic show.

"OK. How about this? Let's say they are still here, and we'll start covering all our bases," said Lieutenant Glen understanding Bobby's reaction. "Have you spoken to that Gary person from the farm lately? Things have been too quiet. Go talk to Jessie and Mae again. There has to be something. Keep your eyes open for some wet roads. I'm not kidding."

"OK. I'm on my way out to the farm. I understand everything but the 'wet road' part." Bobby walked out the office. As he headed for the main doors to leave the building, he stopped and looked at the clock on the wall and then his watch, then he walked out of the building. As Bobby walks to the car, he couldn't stop thinking about what the boy said about him having a secret. He had been thinking about something, but hadn't told anyone, when the boy said that. How did he know?

***

As Bobby was driving down the driveway to the breeding barn, he saw Jessie's truck. Good I'm glad he's here, Bobby thought. When he got to the barn, he saw Mae was with Jessie. He had hoped to speak with Jessie alone. Mae was fine, but she looked so upset from talking about the case. Jessie didn't act like he liked Bobby's company anyway, but with Mae there it was like he was protecting her. Bobby got out of his car.

"Hello, Jessie and Miss Mae. How are we this morning?" Bobby was trying to be as friendly as he could. It had been a strange morning. Jessie looked so tired, and Mae didn't look much better. "What's wrong?" Bobby asked with concern.

Jessie looked at Bobby, holding back tears. "They said we have a ten-day notice, and then we don't have a job. We just got the word from Mr. Hunter a minute ago. He just left."

"Did he say why? Any reason whatsoever?" Bobby was looking around the inside of the barn.

"He said it was because we let 'that girl' stay here. He knew Scout was here because we asked him if she could be here. We never said she was living here though. Scout just needed help. We never dreamed it would turn into this."

"What about Gary? Have you seen him? Does he still work here?" Bobby was confused.

"We haven't seen him in two days. He hasn't been on the farm. I talked to the girls who pick out the stalls in the training barn. They told me that Mr. Hunter was talking to him and then he walked out, got in his truck, and was gone. He never even came back for his clothes. At least that's what they told me." Jessie stopped for a moment, looked at Mae, then looked back at Bobby. "You know, Bobby...I can call you 'Bobby,' right? It's OK?" Bobby, looking a little puzzled, nodded his head. "Well, Mr. Hunter owns the house we live in. You don't think he'll make us move in ten days, do you? Where would we go?"

"Hold on, Jessie. Let me go see the Hunters. Maybe I can find out what is going on. I'll be back. If you're gone, I'll come by the house. If that's OK?"

"Sure. Come on by. Nothing like having company when you're getting kicked out of your house."

"He hasn't kicked you out yet. Let me go see if I can talk to him."

As Bobby walked away, he looked back at Jessie and said, "If no one has seen Gary, does anyone else know where Scout is? Please say yes."

Jessie just shook his head. "No. Gary was the only one who knew those people."

Bobby just tossed his hands in the air and said, "Add something else to the list." He walked to his car, opened the door, got in, sat for a few minutes, started it up, and drove away.

"Do you think Scout is OK?" Mae was looking deeply into Jessie's soul to make sure he wasn't telling her a lie.

"I don't know Mae, but I sure hope so. I really do."

"I think she's good—or I'd feel it. I know I'd feel it." Tears were coming down her face. Jessie held her while tears fell down his face too.

***

Bobby walked up to the main house and knocked on the door, not sure what he was going to say. A young woman answered the door. "Can I help you?"

"Is Mr. and Mrs. Hunter in? My name is Sergeant Carson, with the police department."

"They aren't here. They've gone on vacation out of the country. I'm not sure where they went. They said they'd be back in a week or two."

Bobby stood there, looking at her, thinking, This poor girl has never had a life.

"Well, do you know where I could find Gary, the horse trainer?" Bobby wanted to find *somebody*.

"No. I don't like horses and have nothing to do with them."

Thank you for letting all that personality shine, Bobby thought. "Thank you, miss. Would you give the Hunters and Gary my card if you see them and have them give me a call? It's very important." He handed her a couple of cards and walked away.

How could they be gone so quickly when he just told Jessie today he had ten days and then he would have to go get another job. Something didn't seem right. Bobby walked around the side of the house. The garage doors were open, and there was a car in every spot. Bobby had never met the Hunters. Every time he wanted to talk to them, they sent their attorney.

It just seemed odd that they didn't want to talk. The people at the other farm did with no problem. Something just wasn't right. And where was Gary? What part in this did he have other than being the only one who knew where Scout was? This wasn't working into a pretty picture in Bobby's head.

***

Back at the breeding barn, Jessie was walking around checking stalls to make sure they had plenty of water and the stalls were clean. Mae was sweeping out the tack room and the feed room. There was one mare in the barn that had a cut on her leg that needed tending to. Jessie grabbed a halter, put it on the mare, and led her to Mae. She took the lead line while Jessie went to get some clean bandages. When Jessie opened the door to get the bandages, an envelope fell to the ground with his name on it.

He opened it, and it said, *Phone number for Scout. Please do not tell anyone or give it to anyone.* It had to be from Gary. Jessie put the note in his pocket, got some bandages, and headed back to where Mae was holding the mare. He replaced the bandage and put the mare back up. "Come on, Mae. Let's go home and take a break before we have to feed."

"But what about Sergeant Carson? He said he would be back."

"He also said, if we weren't here, he'd come by the house. Now, come on. Let's go."

"OK, I'm coming." They both got into the truck and drove away.

Bobby drove by a short time later and saw the truck was gone. Must have gone home for lunch, he thought. Bobby stopped by their house and told them that the Hunters weren't at home and if they had any contact with the Hunters to please let him know. They said they would, and Bobby went back to the office to make some calls.

Chapter 6

JUST ANOTHER SCHOOL

Living with the Blake family a few days had been nice. Their place was something. I hadn't been off the farm much, with no need to go anywhere. We rode horses every day. I've learned so much. It's been great—no one asking me any questions about what happened. That was nice. I needed a break.

This morning was different. Mrs. Blake said I needed to go to school. I heard them talking about it the other day. So today was the day. I hated school, but I do what I'm told. Just to be able to come back here would be worth it.

I looked at Jim and the other four heads on the side of the bed and said, "Back to school today. I'll miss you all. Jim, please stay out of trouble."

The smell of breakfast was in the air, grabbing me and pulling me in. I put my clothes on and headed into the kitchen. Frankie, the youngest boy, commented, "Is that all you have to wear, Little Sister? You've worn that and that one other pair of pants and shirt ever since you got here."

"Does it look bad, Little Brother?" I asked, knowing my face was as red as it could be.

"No, it looks fine. You always look fine. I think you're the prettiest big sister anyone could have."

"Frankie is right; you do need some more clothes," said Mrs. Blake. "Today after school, we'll go shopping. Nothing wrong with what you have, but it wouldn't hurt to have some extra."

"We all don't have to go, do we?" said Mike, the other boy, just older than Frankie. "I have plenty of clothes."

"No. It will just be Scout and me—kind of like a girls' afternoon out. What do you think, Scout?"

"Sounds like fun, but I don't have any money to pay for new clothes."

"No worries. Oh, I can't wait! Going shopping with someone other than Grandma will be fun."

I had never seen Mrs. Blake *unhappy*, but, boy, she sure could get *happy*. It was fun to watch—and contagious. Everyone was happy. Nice! I liked this. Everyone but me grabbed a book bag and walked out. With big grins on their faces, and in harmony, all four boys said, "See you at school, Little Sister."

Mrs. Blake planned to take me to get signed in at the school and introduced me to the principal. They didn't have any of my records, but somehow Mrs. Blake got me into the school.

Another new day. What could go wrong?

As Mrs. Blake and I were fixing to leave, all the dogs were standing by the door. I looked at them and said, "All you be good today, and stay out of trouble. See you this afternoon." And with that, they turned and ran to the barn, where everyone was getting ready for the day. "Thanks a lot, dogs. I'll miss you too." The dogs barked but kept on running to the barn—even Jim. That hurt my feelings a little.

"Come on, Scout. Let's go," Mrs. Blake said. She was already getting in the car. I got in. Inside was a book bag. Mrs. Blake looked at me and said, "That one is yours. You like it?"

"Yes, of course!" It was a book bag with a picture of a border collie on it, which looked just like Jim. How could I not like it? We arrived at the school after the bell rang for everyone to go to class. We drove up front and parked. I could feel the eyes of the other children, who could see us from the classrooms. We got out and walked right on into the building and straight for the main office. Mrs. Blake knew exactly where she was going. I bet she had been here at time or two. When we walked into the office, she pointed for me to sit down. I did, and she proceeded into the principal's office.

As I waited one of the assistants asked, "What did you do to make Mrs. Blake come in here?"

"Nothing," I said. "This is just my first day."

"Are you related to the Blake family?"

"No—just visiting for a while. Don't know how long I'll be here." The office door opened, and Mrs. Blake and Principal Henry came walking out. "Scout, this is Principal Henry."

"Hello," I said, not knowing anything else to say.

"Caroline will be taking you to your class.

Caroline, please take Scout here to Mr. Wallace's class. He has her class schedule with him. Thank you." Mrs. Blake looked at me and said, "Have a good day, my child."

"OK. Bye!" I said, feeling a little lost. But with the way things had been, lost was starting to feel normal.

While walking to the classroom, Caroline asked all kinds of questions. Where was I from? How did I know the Blakes? "We don't get many newcomers here. Well, we have a lot of tourists in the summer. Not many stay. You going to be staying for a while?"

"Don't know," I answered.

We got to the classroom, which was the worst part—walking in as the new kid, saying your name and where you're from. What would I say? Well, anything would be better than listening to this Caroline woman blab away.

I walked into the classroom, ready for anything.

"Everyone, this is my sister, Scout. She'll be coming to school here with us. Please be kind because she is my best sister." Coming from John, that was awesome. It made me blush.

"Welcome to my class, Scout. My name is Mr. Wallace."

"She sure doesn't look like your sister, John. She's a White girl; you're an Indian. How can she be your sister, boy?"

"That's enough of that, Sam! I will hear no more of it. Do you hear me? Why have you gotten such a mean streak in you lately?" When Mr. Wallace said it, he realized that maybe something was going on and dropped the subject. Everyone became quiet in the classroom.

"Scout, please, come sit here." Mr. Wallace was pointing at a desk next to John. Most teachers wouldn't do that–put you next to someone you know–but I'm sure glad he did.

John looked at me and winked. "Got you covered, Sis," he whispered.

"Thanks," I said.

I didn't know what class this was until I looked up and saw math problems on the board. I hate math.

✳ ✳ ✳

The rest of the morning was uneventful. Then came lunch. None of the boys were in my last class, so I was on my own going to find the lunchroom. Mrs. Blake had fixed me some lunch, so all I had to do was find somewhere to sit. I was hoping to find John or Tommy but wasn't successful. Maybe they had lunch at a different time? I walked outside and saw a bench by a tree, so I headed that way. I sat down and pulled out my lunch. It was a chicken sandwich, a pickle, chips, and a frozen lemonade, which kept everything nice and cold. I was just fixing to take a bite of my sandwich when Willy popped into my head...

"Look out, Scout!" was the last thing I remembered, except the fact that Willy was still with me. He was telling me all about what it was like to be where he was now...that he was OK, and no one was hurting him anymore.

He asked me, "Why did you care about me so much? No one else would have cried for me like you did, and your heart is so good. Why me?"

"You're a good person, Willy. I don't know why you mean so much to me...Am I dead, Willy?"

"No. It's not your time yet. I will take care of you. You'll be OK. Just don't believe in death right now. If you give up, I can't help you. Do you understand?"

"I think so," I answered, not knowing what else to say. We took long walks through grassy fields–horses everywhere...dogs, cats... even cows, pigs. I even saw an elephant. I thought to myself, This is crazy! And the whole time, Willy just looked at me and smiled.

"These are the things that make you happy, so these are the things that will make you well," Willy said to me. Well, one thing was for sure: it made me happy seeing Willy smile. I didn't know how long it had been when Willy said, "Scout, time to wake up. Come on, girl. You have to go now. There will be another time, but you have to wake up now."

Sharp pains shot through my head and body. I felt this way before. Was everything a dream? Was I back home with my brothers? Had they beaten me up again? Tears started coming down my face, as I thought everything was just a dream.

"Scout, Scout, please wake up! Please!" I could feel a little hand holding mine. I opened my eyes, and it was Frankie. He was crying so hard, and I was crying too–but now because it dawned on me that maybe it *wasn't* all a dream. "Grandma, Grandma!" I could hear Frankie running down a hallway.

Tommy walked into the room. "I'm so sorry, Scout, that we weren't there for you. Do you know who did this to you?"

"The chicken sandwich is the last thing I remember. How long have I been out?"

"Just a couple of hours...Who is Willy?"

"That is her caretaker from the other side, Tommy. Hi, Scout. I'm Winnie, or Grandma, whichever works for you. And I'm your caretaker on *this* side."

"Grandma, sometimes I worry about you–'this side...that side,'" Tommy said.

"You know what I'm talking about Tommy. You've been there. You've seen it. You'll be a caretaker one day also, my sweet Tommy."

"What happened? I don't remember anything," I said.

"Well, you were found all beat up and out cold," Tommy started saying, but Grandma stopped him.

"You need to rest, my child. We'll talk later."

"OK." And that was the last of me. I fell asleep.

* * *

"Wake up, Scout. Wake up. You've had enough rest for right now. I need to give you some medicine," Grandma said.

"Where am I?" I tried to look around. "Where is everyone? Do I know you? I do, don't I? What happened? Why do I hurt so much?"

"OK. Let's start with me. I am Winnie or Grandma, whichever you choose. You were at school fixing to eat lunch, and someone hit you in the back of the head with something. Someone found you and called 911. You went screaming off in an ambulance. Can I assume you don't remember any of this? They ran tests, x-rays, and I don't know what else. But they said you will be OK—with some rest and someone keeping an eye on you. That's where I come in. I'm Grandma, and I'm here to keep an eye on you. Do you want some soup?"

"Where's Jim?" At the sound of his name, Jim jumped up onto the bed.

"He hasn't left your side, my dear."

"Where am I?"

"You're at my house so I can watch you. My daughter has too much to do, with four boys and that farm to help look after. So you'll be here with me for a few days. It will be nice having someone here.

You feel like sitting up and tasting a little soup? These meds they're giving you say you have to eat something."

As I was trying to sit up in bed, I suddenly realized—"I need to go to the bathroom please."

"I will help you. Just take it slow."

This lady put her arms around me, and, for a grandma, she felt like she could carry me if needed. She made me feel safe. She took all the fear out of me when her arms were around my shoulders. It was like she was feeding me strength. She was a tall lady and had long, straight hair and the kindest eyes I had ever seen. After the bathroom, she took me right back to bed. She helped me get all propped up, and she set a tray in front of me with a bowl of soup. The fumes from that soup filled my nose with delight. I took one spoonful to my mouth, and my whole body tasted it. It felt like it ran from my head down to my toes, then out to my hands. Before I knew it, it was gone. I looked at Grandma and said, "More, please?"

"Just a little more. Don't want you getting well too fast—I like the company." Grandma went to get one more bowl. "Here you go, but this is it for right now. You may have some later." The second bowl went faster than the first.

My body wasn't hurting like it had.

Grandma said, "Lie back and rest. I'll be back in a little while. You'll be feeling better soon."

I don't remember putting my head on the pillow, but I was soon asleep.

* * *

When I woke the next time, it was dark. I was confused and couldn't keep things straight in my head. Had I been dreaming? There was no way soup tasted that good. Someone walked into the room. It was so dark that I couldn't see my hand in front of my face.

"Is that you Winnie…Grandma?" I asked, not sure what to call her.

"'Grandma' is fine, my child."

"Why is it so dark in here?"

"Don't use my lights. People are so used to convenient things that they lose most of the senses that are in all of us. To me, turning on the lights at night is like wearing blinders during the day. Sitting in the dark, you can look inside yourself and learn about yourself with no interruptions. If people would sit in the dark and talk to each other, they would realize we are all the same.

"Young, old, black, white, brown—I am you, and you are me. We aren't different. Anyone who thinks color, size, weight, or age makes us different is never going to know what truth is. Time and space are irrelevant; Einstein taught us that. Our past, our future, and our now make us who we are. You are my child, and I am your ancestors, child. Good, bad, or different—we are all one and the same. So if we would talk at night in the dark, people could hear better and not make judgments because of looks."

As she was talking, it all made sense. I could hear the words and see the words and feel the words. It didn't matter who was saying them. It was a very peaceful way of communicating. Being in the dark just made it clearer. "You feel like getting up?" Grandma asked.

"I think so. I feel pretty good really. But I cannot see a thing."

"It's OK. I will guide you. Here, just hold my hand." We walked outside, and she set me down in a chair. "Look up, Scout." It was so dark, and the sky was lit up like the Fourth of July. It was always pretty when I stayed in that barn—but nothing like this. "Wow! This is crazy! I've looked at the stars before, but they've never looked like this. What did you do? Do you know magic?"

"This is what I've been trying to tell you about man-made light. It keeps you from being able to see." A shooting star ripped across the sky, and then another one.

"Holy crap! I mean...I'm sorry, but that was awesome!"

Grandma had her arm around me, and I lay against her and thought to myself, I sure do like it here...I wish Willy could see this.

Grandma looked down at me and said, "He does."

Chapter 7

GOT MILK

Bobby walked into his office and saw a note to go see Lieutenant Glen.

He knocked on the Lieutenant's door and then walked in.

"Good morning, Bobby. How are you this morning?"

"I'm OK. No new answers, just more questions. No one has seen that trainer boy–Gary was his name–and they said the Hunters have gone out of town, but no cars are missing. The only person who will talk to me is the attorney, and he has nothing to say."

"Has Jessie heard from them?"

"Not since he fired them–ten days, then they don't have a job. You know the Hunters own that house they live in. What will they do? And there is no information on Scout. No telling what's going on with her. In other words, I have no good news, if you can call any of that news."

A lady walked into the office and informed Sergeant Carson that there was a bad traffic accident on Idlewild Road.

"Are horse trailers involved?"

"Not that I know of, but they are asking for you to come."

"OK, on my way. Send the directions to my GPS in the car. Who is there now?"

"That Johnny Walker young boy, who just started."

"Send him some backup. I'm on my way."

"Yes, sir." Then the lady was gone.

"See you later, Lieutenant Glen. Duty calls."

"Bobby, be careful."

"What is that all about?" Bobby said to himself as he walked out of the office.

Bobby got to his car and turned on the GPS to see where this accident was exactly. Idlewild Road was a long, two-lane road that many trucks used. Bobby picked up the radio and called the young boy on duty. "Officer Walker, how bad of an accident is this?"

"Well, sir, it's the worst wreck I've ever seen. A tanker truck and a concrete truck were fighting for the same lane but going in two different directions."

"Was anyone hurt?"

"They said everyone will be OK; the ambulance is here now."

"What kind of tanker truck is it?"

"It's a tanker full of milk. There's milk all over the road. The milk is still coming out of the trailer." Bobby sat there for a minute, then Johnny came back on the radio. "Did you copy that, Serge?"

"Yes, I'm here. Are there any other vehicles on the road?"

"Fire trucks, ambulances, and some first responders."

"Listen to me, son," Bobby said, trying to stay calm. "You get everyone out of the road. Do you hear me? Get them out of the road. Something bad is fixing to happen. Get everyone out of the road, *now!* I'm on my way."

Before the young man could answer, Bobby heard him yell, "Oh shit!" And that was the last he heard. Then the police radio was all abuzz—everyone calling for backup and more ambulances. Bobby turned on the blue light and drove as fast as he could. But he wasn't ready to see what had just happened.

As Bobby got closer to the scene, he could see that it was a really bad accident. The sounds as he got closer were deafening. All he could hear were screams—screams from people, screams from horses. There were cars, trucks, trailers, and ambulances scattered everywhere. The white milk on the road was a dirty pink color. Smells began taking over the air around him—the smell of the dead and the dying. In the distance he could hear the sirens of emergency vehicles coming his way. Here comes the cavalry, he thought. When he got out of his car, it was a lot to take in. A fire truck had been knocked over onto the sidewalk, where people had been standing watching the first wreck; the first responders for the first wreck were now victims themselves. Now, all of the new crews were there in overdrive.

The horses—Bobby was trying to get to the trailers to see if any were alive. The horses were in total crazy mode. One trailer was on its side, and people were trying to get the horses out. Bobby's better judgment was to tell them to stop because they could get hurt, but in the moment he would take all the help he could get.

He called Jessie, and when Jessie answered the phone, Bobby told him, "Jessie, I need your help, but you cannot bring Mae. There's been an accident, and I really need your help. Here are the directions...Oh, and please call a veterinarian or two; we could sure use them."

"I'm on my way," Jessie told Bobby, with a panicked sound in his voice, before hanging up. "Now, Mae, I got to go, and you need to stay here, please. I need you to call some of the veterinarians that we use and give them this address...Please no arguments." From Jessie's look, Mae knew she had to stay.

"I'll call the veterinarians and give this location. Please be careful, Jessie."

"Thank you, Mae, I'll call you as soon as I know what's going on." Jessie put on his boots and grabbed his jacket, then walked out the door.

Bobby made his way to the cab of the first truck. There was a EMT standing there, and when Bobby looked at him, he just shook his head to say no one was alive. When Bobby looked at the mangled bodies, it was clear. He almost got sick.

A older EMT with a bald head and a cap on, he had blood all over him. He did what he could do in that truck and grabbed his bag and started walking. Bobby followed.

Bobby and the EMT made their way to the second truck, stepping over bits and pieces of vehicles and other things that Bobby didn't want to think about. He couldn't hear the screams anymore; he had to block them out. As they were making their way to the second truck, some people were trying to open the trailer door. This trailer wasn't on its side, but the horses were on top of each other, stomping and screaming. It was enough to make you want to run away. They finally reached the truck cab. The EMT opened the driver's side of the truck cab and saw what was left of a man leaning over the steering wheel, his face in the windshield.

"No hope for him," the EMT said With very little expression. It was like he did this everyday. Bobby wondered how he could be so calm. This was awful. Bobby was having a hard time holding it together.

A man in the passenger seat was on the floor of the truck, in a ball. When they reached for him, they realized he was tied up. There was blood all over him. When they tried to move him, they heard him moan.

"Oh my god. This man's still alive" the EMT said. "This man's alive!" he yelled to some other paramedics. They came running, untied him, and put him in an ambulance. He was gone.

Jessie arrived shortly after and couldn't believe what he was seeing. Bobby saw him drive up and made his way over to him. "Do you think these are the horses that were stolen?" Bobby asked Jessie.

Jessie was in shock. He had never seen anything like this before. The noise of hurt and dying horses and people, the smells, and the pink sour milk were enough to make you sick. With tears in his eyes, Jessie looked and Bobby, then walked away to throw up. Bobby followed him and tried to comfort him the best he could.

By this time, one of the veterinarians had arrived and was on the phone calling for more help. Jessie pulled himself back together and looked at Bobby and said, "I have to go help the veterinarian. I'll let you know something soon." Jessie started walking away, then turned around and said, "Bobby, thank you for telling me to make Mae stay home. This would have been too much for her." But as Jessie headed to help, he thought, This is too much for me.

Bobby got into his car and headed to the hospital to see who the survivor was that was in that truck. If that autistic boy was right, Bobby would be able to get some answers, hopefully, or at least an identity of who this person was and why he was tied up.

On the way to the hospital, Bobby called Lieutenant Glen. He told him what was going on and that he was heading to the hospital. Lieutenant Glen said he would meet him there.

At the hospital, it was chaos—people running everywhere, ambulances coming and going unloading people, and doctors yelling orders out at nurses. Bobby couldn't get anyone to talk to him.

One doctor looked at him and said, "Sir, please. Just get out of here, and let us do our job. If you are looking for someone, come back later, please."

Lieutenant Glen walked in as the doctor was talking to Bobby. "What happened?"

Lieutenant Glen asked. Bobby started telling him all that had happened and about the person in the cab of the truck who was still alive. "Do you know who this person is?" Lieutenant Glen asked Bobby.

"Couldn't tell. He was too bloody to recognize him. That's why I am here."

A doctor came by again and wasn't happy actually quite mean "Get out of our way, now!"

Lieutenant Glen looked at Bobby. "I think he really means it. Let's go and see if we can find out anything else at the accident." Bobby really didn't want to go back there, but they both got in Bobby's car and left.

***

When they got back to the scene, most of the vehicles had been removed, and crews were trying to clean up the street. The horses that had to be put down were still on the side of the road. A young officer walked up to Bobby and said, "Sergeant Carson, all the people who survived have been taken to the hospital, and the animals that can be helped have been moved. There is a truck coming now to pick up the dead horses. It should be here soon." The young officer looked very pale.

"You OK, son?" Lieutenant Glen asked.

"Will be, sir. This was a bad one—never seen anything like this before and hope I never do again."

"Have you seen a tall Black man around here? He was helping the veterinarians." Bobby asked.

"You talking about Jessie?" said the young officer.

"Yes, do you know where he is?"

"Yes, sir. He left with one of the veterinarians with a load of horses. Boy, I tell you what, sir. We couldn't have handled all those horses without him. What a great person he is."

"Do you think you have enough people here? Or do you need more help?" Lieutenant Glen asked, turning green from that sour milk smell.

"Yes, sir. We have some fire trucks coming to wash down the streets. Maybe the smell will go away. The dead horses are getting pretty rank also. But I think we got this."

"You're doing a great job," Lieutenant Glen said. Then he looked at Bobby and said, "Let's go and see if we can find Jessie. I want to know if these are the stolen horses." They both got into Bobby's car and drove away.

Chapter 8

GRANDMA'S HOUSE

It had been a couple of days, and my head was much better. I was still staying at Grandma's house. Everyone called her "Grandma," and she asked me to call her that also if I wanted. It did fit her, and this felt like what a home should feel like—at least, what I *thought* it should feel like.

The house was a small, with two bedrooms and two baths. It was a really old house but with a welcoming feeling. My single bed slept good—a simple bed, nothing fancy.

In fact, nothing in the house was fancy; it just had everything you needed. The kitchen had pots and pans hanging from the ceiling, and Grandma had a lot of them. There was always something cooking on the stove. Sometimes it was food, and other times it was some kind of medicine. People on the island came to get medicine from her. Sometimes she just talked to them, and sometimes she'd cook something up for them or already have it on the shelf.

The outside of the house had bird feeders, squirrel feeders, and bird houses, as well as one big pit for when Grandma cooked on outside. All the shutters on the house were blue, and the rest of the house was white. She had nothing on the windows—no curtains, no blind, or anything. She said, "With curtains and blinds, you can't see what's going on outside, and you miss so much: the sun coming up, the sun going down, the moon, the stars, the birds." They called the nearby water a creek, but it looked like a river. But her house was right there. You could watch the dolphins swim almost any time of day. I really liked the dolphins, and I really liked this place.

I hadn't gone back to school yet, but they said soon. Tommy was trying to find out what happened to me and who did it. So I'd see.

I did miss the horses, though, so maybe next week I'd go back to riding. The boys would be home soon from school, and they always stopped by. I looked forward to seeing them.

John and Mike walked in from school.

"Where are Tommy and Frankie?" Grandma asked.

"Frankie had to stay after school today, because he's in the Thanksgiving play this year. So Tommy decided to stay till he got done, then bring him home," Mike said. "Scout, today we found out who bopped you on the head," John said, with a big grin on his face.

"Well, tell us. And why are you grinning?" Grandma looked a little confused.

"Well, Grandma, since Scout is OK, it is kind of good news. No one meant to hurt her. There is this boy who did not make it on the baseball team. He was mad and threw a rock at a tree near where Scout was sitting, and hit her in the head by accident. He went to the principal today and confessed. So now Scout can come back to school, right?"

"I guess. What did your parents say?"

"The principal called them, and Mom went in to talk to them about what happened. I thought maybe Mom had talked to you, Grandma, about what happened?"

"No, not yet. But that's OK. It has been a busy day. I will talk to her later, but that's good news. What do you think, Scout?"

I was sitting on the floor, petting Jim. "I'm glad no one meant to hurt me. And school is not that bad, and I guess there is no way out of it, so all is good. I'm ready to go back to school." I looked up with a smile on my face, and Mike and John were smiling also.

Tommy came walking in with Frankie. Grandma said, "Boys, why are you here? John said that Frankie was in the Thanksgiving play. I know practice takes longer than that."

Frankie ran over and jumped in my lap. He put his arms around my neck and burrowed his head under my chin and said, "I don't want to be no tree. Dogs pee on trees. Don't want to be no tree."

"There you go, Grandma. Can't argue with that. No one could win that one, so he is no longer in the play. I wish I could have come up with that when they made me be in that stupid play," Tommy said, grinning from ear to ear.

"Well, your mom and dad can handle this one. I never thought that play was all that great anyway. Never understood why anyone would want a child to be a plant," Grandma said looking down at Frankie, who was looking up at Grandma with a smile knowing she wasn't upset with him.

"I love you, Grandma," Frankie said as he jumped up and ran to hug grandma.

"Tommy, go see if your mom and dad want to go to the beach tonight. It is going to be a full moon. I think Scout would like to see it," Grandma said.

"Can we eat dinner on the beach too?" Tommy said all excited.

"Yes. I have it all ready to go. Now, go see if your mom and dad want to go. I think it's going to be a great night on the beach."

You couldn't have stopped Tommy with a shotgun. He was out the door and gone. Everyone else gathered things together: chairs, blankets, and baskets that Grandma loaded with food.

I looked at John and said, "How do you know your mom and dad are going to want to go the beach?"

"When grandma says it is a good night to be at the beach, no way would our mom and dad say no. They'll be here before we finish packing. You just wait and see."

And John was right. Before we could get everything packed up, Tommy was back with their mom and dad. They had baskets of food, chairs, blankets, and all the dogs. Before I knew it, we were off to the beach. I'd never been to the beach. It wasn't dark yet; the sun was still up. I was so excited because everyone else was, but I had no idea what was to come.

We drove up to this place with sand everywhere. I didn't see any water. It looked like desert pictures I had seen. They let the dogs loose, and the dogs just took off. Jim looked at me and then followed the others.. "Come on, Scout." Frankie had me by the hand, tugging as hard as he could. He pulled me toward a sandy knoll that the dogs had run over. Jim came running back over the knoll, wet and sandy but really happy. He was so excited that he couldn't stand himself.

As we were walking off, I heard "Frankie, you and Scout aren't going empty-handed. We have a lot of stuff here. Grab something please."

"OK. Sorry. I forgot," Frankie said with that sweet smile of his. Grandma just sat back and took it all in. Like it was the best day she ever saw. I grabbed some chairs. Frankie grabbed one of the food baskets (not surprising). Everyone got an armful and headed over that knoll. Grandma brought up the rear with the blankets and a look of total peace and contentment. She knew where she belonged. She just sat back and took it all in, like it was the best day she ever saw. That had to be a special feeling, I thought.

As we walked over the knoll, I had to stop. It was amazing: the water, the smell, the dogs running up and down. It was like water in the middle of a desert. This was crazy. This was amazing. This was…I couldn't find the words. It was too overwhelming. Grandma put her arm around me, looked me straight in the eyes, and said, "Child, welcome to my world. Come on. There is a lot to see. Just wait. You haven't seen anything yet."

I couldn't imagine that there could be anything more; this was the best place ever. I looked up at Grandma and said, "Thank you for letting me come to your world…because my world wasn't good. So thank you."

"Everyone is welcome to my world, and my world will spit you out if you don't belong. And, my little friend Scout, you belong here. This is now your world." Grandma looked at me with a tear in her eyes.

I knew she meant every word, and all I could say was, "Thank you."

"Come on, Scout." Tommy was waving his hands, standing in that strange water. I'd never seen water that looked like that. And all the shells, sand, and water—it was just too crazy.

Grandma said, "Go put your stuff down, and start a new adventure. Have fun, my child."

I set the chairs down, looked at Tommy's mom, and said, "I know you aren't my mom or dad, but I feel strange calling you anything else because that is all I hear. Do you think that's OK?"

Mom stopped in her tracks, looked at me with tears running down her cheeks, grabbed me, and said, holding me tight, "I always wanted a daughter. You would sure make my day. Thank you so much."

"Can I call you Dad? Would that be OK?" I said turning to Dad.He just nodded his head and smiled. He couldn't get near me because Mom wouldn't let go. It felt so good.

Well, that didn't last long. Suddenly, Mike and Frankie had me by both arms, and off we went toward that strange-looking water. Jim was so excited that he could run, here and there, in and out of the water; it was like he couldn't stop. The other dogs were doing the same, and all that excitement was contagious.

As we got close to the water, we stopped. Everyone sat down, took off their shoes, and rolled up their pants, so I did the same. The next thing I knew, were running up and down the beach in this strange water. The water would curl up and fall down. It had some kind of foam that would line the sand. It tasted like salt, and it went as far as I could see. It was the best place ever. We ran, playing tag or rolling in the sand, which I regretted a little later on. But this was the best day ever.

Grandma had gone walking down the beach. She'd been out of sight for a good while. She came walking back and signaled for everyone to come to her. Mom, Dad, the dogs, and the rest of us went running toward her.

"It's time," she said.

The sun was starting to go down. Grandma started walking at a quick pace. It was hard keeping up without having to trot along. She stopped. The sun was a big, red ball fixing to fall into the ocean. Grandma squatted down, looking at the sand, which was moving and caving into itself.

"What's going on?" I asked Tommy.

"Just wait" is all he said.

As we sat there watching, this little creature came crawling out… then another…and many more. I reached to grab one, but John grabbed my hand to stop me.

"Just watch; don't touch," Grandma said.

There must have been hundreds. "What are they?" I asked.

"Sea turtles!" cried Frankie. "Come on. We can't touch, but we can help." Frankie ran alongside the turtles chasing the birds away. And there were birds everywhere. Frankie and Mike were swinging their hands in the air, shooing the birds away. I couldn't help it; I had to join them, with Jim at my side. We chased the birds, and the little turtles got in the water, while the ocean was eating up the big, red sun.

After the last turtle went into the water, we headed back to where we had our spot. Mom had the blankets, food, chairs, and plates laid out. It was almost completely dark at this time. We sat down, and I talked about the turtles, while eating fried chicken, potato salad, and fruit. Boy, life was good. But then it got dark.

The ocean started spitting out the moon, which was as red as the sun when it went down. It was huge; it took up the whole sky. It was so bright that the stars couldn't shine.

Tommy looked at me and said, "Come with me. I want to show you something."

Everyone got up and headed to the water. Tommy ran out and kicked the water. It looked like fire; the water was glowing. It looked like it was going to eat him up. He picked up the water and let it fall through his fingers, and it would sparkle bright sparkles. It was incredible. Mom, Dad, Mike, and Frankie, along with Tommy and Grandma—we all were playing in this crazy, amazing water.

It got a little cold after the sun went down, but no one cared. Mike had water falling through his hands and—There was Willy. He had a huge smile, and I heard him say, "Looking good, my friend. You deserve this moment." Then he was gone.

Grandma put her arm around me and said, "He looks at peace and pleased."

"You saw him too?"

"No. I felt him. I know he's here with you. You're a lucky child."

"Why can you not see him, Grandma?" I asked, a little tearful.

"Honey, I'll explain later. Right now, have fun, and know he is happy for you." Grandma was right.

After a while, we all were tired, so we loaded up the truck and headed back home. When we got back, they dropped Grandma off and said I could come back to the house if I wanted. I asked to stay one more night at Grandma's. Mom was OK with that, and so I got out of the truck too.

As I was getting ready for bed, I went to Grandma and asked, "Can we go outside for a while and talk? Please, Grandma?" She smiled at me and said, "Sure. Let's go. Do you want some hot chocolate? It's a little chilly out there."

"Yes, that would be great." We sat in the swing for a while before I could ask the questions on my mind, but I had to know. "Grandma, how do you know when Willy is around? And why can't you see him?"

"Well, my child, it is like this: You knew Willy when he was in human form, so when he comes to you, that's how you see him. I didn't know him then, so when his spirit comes to see you, I can hear him and feel his presence. That is what spirits are; they are all a face to someone. But not everyone can see. Understand what I'm trying to say? Have you ever felt spirits around you?"

"Yes!" I said with great excitement. "I have, but I thought I was crazy because I couldn't see them—just hear and feel them. That makes so much sense. So I'm not strange? My real brothers would beat me up and call me crazy. I think my parents thought that also."

"My dear, your real brothers are Tommy, John, Mike, and Frankie. They love you, and they are your real brothers. They will always be there for you. Never let them hear you say they aren't your real brothers—because they are."

"Really, Grandma? Are you sure? I feel like I'm in a dream and am going to wake up back in that nightmare." Sudden sadness took over me; I couldn't go back to that. I hadn't let myself think about this much, but after tonight I didn't think I could handle that.

"I can't make any promises. But if things get bad, you now have something to work for. You know where you belong. Things won't be wonderful all the time, but now you have these wonderful memories to help you through whatever you are going through. You'll always have a home here. Never forget that. I know a little about why you're here—but not much. It will all work out, but I can't foresee the future. But I know, sooner or later, you'll have to go back. For how long or when that will be, I have no idea. Just know you belong here. But for right now, let's just enjoy the good times."

Grandma looked down at me and saw that I was asleep. Grandma was glad I fell asleep. Maybe tonight wasn't the night to say these things. I had such a great time on the beach—no need to take that away.

Grandma thought: Sleep, my little friend. Sleep with wonderful dreams. We will deal with reality later.

Grandma tried waking me up so she could get me to bed. I fell into the bed and never moved. Grandma covered me up and let Jim jump up on the bed with me.

"Sleep tight, my little friend. Protect her in her dreams, Jim. You're a special little dog. Stay close to her. Don't let her stray." Jim jumped up and licked Grandma as if to say, "No worries. I got this."

Grandma walked out in the dark, never turning on a light.

Chapter 9

MAN IN THE TRUCK

Jessie was sitting in Lieutenant Glen's office drinking some iced tea. Lieutenant Glen walked in and sat behind his desk.

"It's been a couple of weeks since the accident with those horses. Can you tell me with full certainty that some of those horses are the ones stolen from the farm you work at, Jessie?"

"Didn't Bobby tell you? The Hunters fired me. I don't have a job right now, and Mae went back to cleaning more houses. As far as the horses go, all of them are the Hunters' horses."

"What? What are you talking about, Jessie? When did the Hunters let you go? And *why*?" Lieutenant Glen's face was turning redder by the second. "When did you know that those horses were the Hunters'? Did Bobby know this?" Bobby Carson are you here?" Lieutenant Glen yelled out the door, "Bobby Carson, are you here?"

The secretary at the desk looked at him and said, "No, he's not here. He's gone to the hospital to check on that man who was in the truck."

"Lieutenant Glen, calm down please," Jessie said. "Bobby didn't know about the horses; I just found out for sure myself. I may not be working for the Hunters, but the few horses that lived are staying with the veterinarian over in the next town. I've been helping him with them. Only eight survived, and they were so beat up. And then those that didn't make it...I had to go and recheck them to be sure. It wasn't an easy task. The horses were a mess, and I'd known most of them all their lives. But I had to be sure." Jessie stopped for a minute so Lieutenant Glen could catch up.

Lieutenant Glen looked a little out of sorts but was coming around. "Jessie, where are you living?" Lieutenant Glen went from anger to concern.

"I'm looking for something but haven't found anything yet. The Hunters didn't say I had to move out yet. I think they just wanted me off the farm because Mr. Hunter knew I could recognize his horses if they were caught. And when he finds out that I know and told you, he will have us out in a skinny second." Jessie looked scared. He knew this was true, but it didn't seem real till he heard himself say it out loud.

"If this is true, Jessie, then why would he have his own horses stolen?"

"I don't know. I just know that these are his horses."

"What about the horses on that other farm that were stolen? They were on those trailers too."

"Those horses were mares leased from the Hunters' farm. I remember them picking them up. Did anyone ask the people at the other farm whose horses they were?"

"No. I guess we just assumed that those people had owned them. They never indicated that they did not own them." Lieutenant Glen was feeling like a rookie who had just been played. "Has anyone seen or heard from that trainer—Gary, I think his name was?"

"No," Jessie said. "Do you know who that man is in the hospital?" Jessie asked. "Or who the drivers were?"

Lieutenant Glen replied, "The two drivers were some drug runners, and the one passenger who did not survive was a girlfriend of one of the drivers, the best we could tell. Not sure who she was or why she was with them. Jessie, do you know where that little girl is?

Gary was the only one who knew where she went, and now we aren't sure if Gary is involved in this and if that little girl is in danger."

Jessie sat there for a minute before he reached into his pocket, took out the piece of paper with Gary's message, and handed it to Lieutenant Glen. "This was at the farm when I was packing up some things."

Lieutenant Glen unfolded the piece of paper and read it. "Do you think it's from Gary?"

Jessie replied, "He was the only one who knew where she is."

"Did you call her?" Lieutenant Glen asked. "Did you call her, Jessie?"

"No, sir. I was scared to. I feel in my heart that she is OK. I really didn't know what to do, to be honest. Lieutenant Glen, who is the man in the hospital? Does he know anything?"

"Bobby is over there now. The man has been in a coma since the accident. The doctors say that when or if he does wake up, he may not even know who he is, much less what he was tied up for. He had such facial injuries that he is all wrapped up, and no one can even tell what he looks like."

The phone rang, and the receptionist answered. "Yes, Sergeant Carson. Lieutenant Glen is here. Lieutenant Glen, Sergeant Carson on line one."

Lieutenant Glen picked up the phone. "Bobby, any news?"

"Yes, just a little. The man is starting to wake up some, but the doctors say it may be awhile before he'll be able to talk." Bobby was sounding a little flustered.

"Bobby, ride over and ask the Hunters to come in—and to bring their lawyer."

"What do you have in mind?" Bobby asked.

"Just go by and see if they're at home and ask them to come to the police department. I have some questions answered, and I think once I tell the DA what I've found out, they may want to be here also." Lieutenant Glen's mind was in high gear.

Before he hung up, Lieutenant Glen said, "Hey, Bobby, while you're over there, ask around about Gary. See if anybody has heard from him. Actually, do that first because after you confront Mr. and Mrs. Hunter; I'm sure they will ask you to leave. Call me back, and let me know how it goes. Thanks, Bobby. Be careful."

With that, Lieutenant Glen hung up the phone.

Lieutenant Glen now focused on Jessie. "Jessie, I have a little cabin up on the lake, and I want you and Mae to go stay in it till this is over. You need to get all your things out of your house that you want and store them somewhere. Pack some bags and go to this address." Lieutenant Glen started writing directions down on a piece of paper. "When I start questioning the Hunters about those horses, I don't want them coming after you or Mae. There's enough food up there to last you two or three weeks."

Lieutenant Glen started writing directions down on a piece of paper. "What are you saying? Are we in danger?" Jessie looked scared.

"I don't know," said Lieutenant Glen, "but you said that you were able to recognize all those horses as being the Hunters', and the Hunters know that."

"What about Gary? He knows all those horses too."

"Yes, what about Gary? Where is Gary? Do you know?" Lieutenant Glen continued, "I want to know where you and Mae are because I want to keep you safe." Jessie looked really concerned. "Jessie, please, you'll have a couple of days. The Hunters won't come in right away. Don't let anyone know where you are going. I would like it if no one knew you were gone. Do you understand me? Please, I just want to keep you safe."

Jessie could see the look of concern on Lieutenant Glen's face, and he knew he had to listen. "Thank you, Lieutenant Glen. I'll let you know when we get moved in."

"Just let *me* know, not anyone else, Jessie—just for right now. I do not want any slips of the tongue, if you know what I mean. Be careful. And here is my cell number; call this number only."

In shock, Jessie got up, grabbed his coat, and headed out the door. He never thought that this would get this ugly. What had they gotten into?

Bobby drove to the training barn on the Hunters' farm looking for Gary. He got out and walked into the barn, and there was no one to be found. There were horses in the stalls, and they all looked OK, but something just didn't look right. Everything was out of sorts. He walked all the way through the barn. And no one. This is too odd, he thought.

Bobby walked back out to the car and drove to the house. He got to the house, and again no one in sight. The grass had not been mowed. The cars in the garage had not been moved. Something was definitely wrong. Bobby called dispatch and said, "I need backup at this address." Dispatch called out for available cars to respond to Bobby's location. Two patrols responded, and the closest one was eight minutes away.

Bobby walked back around to the front of the house. He walked up to the front door. He rang the doorbell...but nothing. It was just too quiet. He walked around the side of the house and looked into the window, and nothing. Bobby got on his phone and called Lieutenant Glen. "Lieutenant, I'm at the Hunters' house. I've been down to the training barn, and it looks like no one has been around here. Someone must be coming by to feed the horses, but I don't know...it looks pretty deserted."

"Bobby, did you call for backup?"

"Yes, sir—should be at any minute."

"Bobby, just stay there. I'm going to get a search warrant, if I can, and will be on my way. I'll call when I know my ETA."

"OK, Lieutenant. I'll see you when you get here." A patrol car drove up. Bobby walked over to the car told the young officer, "Go over to the hospital, and stand over that man who was in that wreck last week. You know who I'm talking about? He's still in the ICU. Let me know as soon as he is able to talk."

"Yes, sir." And the young officer drove off.

The second officer drove up and got out. "What's going on here, Serge? It's kind of creepy no one is here. Who is feeding the horses and taking care of the place?"

This young officer was a good policeman but looked as though he was not old enough to shave. Bobby has always liked him. "How do you know so much about this place, Officer Franks? I don't recall you being on duty when the horses were stolen." Bobby looked a little suspicious.

"No, sir. I was off duty that night, but my wife is related to the Hunters. Mrs. Hunter is like her aunt on her mother's side. She doesn't talk to them often, but we had our wedding here about five years ago. They had more people here than you could shake a stick at."

"Has your wife talked to the Hunters recently?" Bobby asked.

"Not that I know of. She got a call from Mr. Hunter about four months ago, but that was before all of this happened," Officer Franks, said feeling like he said something wrong.

"Would she come down to the station and talk to me? I need to know more about these people. Would you ask her to meet me there this afternoon?" Bobby was getting anxious.

Officer Franks walked off and called his wife. "Honey, would you stop by the station and talk to my sergeant about your aunt and uncle, the Hunters?"

"When?" she asked.

"This afternoon. What would be a good time for you?"

"I don't want to get involved with whatever they're up to. I'm not close to my aunt and uncle. You know that. The only reason we had our wedding there was because Mom wanted it." She sounds odd, Officer Franks thought. It wasn't like her to avoid things.

"Please, dear. He really needs to talk to you this afternoon."

"OK, OK. Tell him I will be there at three o'clock."

Officer Franks walked back to Bobby said, "She said she'll be there at three o'clock."

* * *

About two hours later, Lieutenant Glen came driving in. He got out of his car and walked over to Bobby. "I couldn't get a warrant, but their attorney said he would meet me here. He should be here any minute." A Mercedes came up the drive.

"Lieutenant Glen, can you handle this from here? I have someone coming to the station who I need to talk to. Officer Franks here—his wife is related to the Hunters, and she agreed to come talk to me at the station at three o'clock. Officer Franks will stay here with you."

"Go, Bobby. I can handle this, and we'll talk later and put our notes together." With that, Bobby got into his car and drove away, without looking at the car that just drove in.

Officer Franks started walking over to the Mercedes when three men got out. Lieutenant Glen was walking around the house to see if he could see anyone or anything. All of the men from the Mercedes had on suits, which made sense since they were lawyers. But something wasn't right. The driver of the car pulled out a gun and shot without hesitation Officer Franks in the forehead. He was dead before he hit the ground. Lieutenant Glen heard the shot—the one and only shot, then silence. The noise from the shot was unmistakable. It was a sound you never forget when you work in law enforcement. He knew this wasn't good. He headed for a shed that was near the pool in the backyard. He got to the shed before a second shot. The shot hit the door behind him. He pulled out his gun and was trying to assess the situation.

The three men were standing in plain view. "You looking for me, Lieutenant Glen? Why are you trespassing on my property? You don't have to worry about your little officer friend. He is unable to help you. You should have stayed at the office. I wanted that Sergeant Carson also, but I see he has left you all alone."

Lieutenant Glen said nothing. No need to talk; they had control of the situation. The three men split up, and Lieutenant Glen knew he was in trouble. One of the three must have been Mr. Hunter, he had never met him but this was a good guess since he was calling all the orders. He was a medium size man, just a little on the chubby size. He had on dark glasses so it was hard to tell what his face looked like.

* * *

Bobby got back to the station and was waiting for this woman to show up, but he had forgotten to ask what her name was. He looked out the office door at the receptionist and said, "Call dispatch and tell them to radio Officer Franks, and get his wife's name for me."

She did as she was told but walked into Bobby's office and said, "They can't reach him. He didn't respond to the call."

Bobby walked out of the office and went straight to dispatch. "Call Lieutenant Glen, and see if Officer Franks is still with him."

Dispatch did as they were told. "No response, Sergeant."

The hair stood up on Bobby's neck. He looked at the lady dispatcher and said, "I'm heading to the Hunters. Send me some backup."

"We already sent two cars out there when you were there.

How many do you need, Sergeant?"

"Send two more. I'm on my way." Bobby raced out of the building, got in his car, turned his lights on, and was on his way. He didn't like this feeling. He wasn't sure what was going on, but he was sure it wasn't good.

* * *

Bobby pulled up in the drive and saw the body on the ground. Very cautiously, he got out of the car. There was only the officer's car and the lieutenant's. Lieutenant Glen was nowhere in sight. Bobby knew he had to wait for backup before going any farther. The other patrol cars were driving up while Bobby was getting a blanket out of the car to cover up Officer Franks. Bobby got on the radio and requested an ambulance.

One of the officers jumped out and said, "Serge, what the hell happened? Is that Jim Franks?"

"Yes, it is. We need to find Lieutenant Glen. He's here somewhere. Be careful. I have no idea what just happened." Bobby started walking around the house when he heard another car driving up the drive. He called to the two officers who were still looking at the body on the ground. "Keep your guard up because I have no idea who that is driving in."

Bobby heard a noise in the bushes at the back of the house. He walked over and realized it was another body. He leaned down and saw that it was Lieutenant Glen. He could hear the ambulance coming down the road. "Lieutenant Glen, can you hear me? Stay with me. Help is on the way." Bobby wasn't sure he was even alive. He felt for a pulse and thought he felt one, but it could have been wishful thinking. He called to the other officers: "Send the paramedics back here." He had panic in his voice. He held the bloody body of his lieutenant.

The paramedics were there before he knew it and told him, "Let him go, sir. We are here. Let us do our job. We got this. Please, sir."

Bobby turned him loose. "He...he still alive?" Bobby asked the paramedic, with a quiver in his voice.

"Yes, but we got to get him out of here now." The paramedics put Lieutenant Glen on a stretcher and headed to the ambulance. The paramedic said to one of the other officers that another ambulance would be here soon to get the other man.

Bobby followed the stretcher to the ambulance and shut the door for them. He looked at a car that drove in after the officers. "Who is that?" he asked.

"He said he's the Hunters' attorney and was supposed to meet Lieutenant Glen here."

Bobby walked over to the car. "You're a little late. I thought you were driving in when I was leaving?"

"No. I was trying to get hold of the Hunters so we could all be here. I told my secretary to give them a call and to tell them to meet us out here. She said she had their cell number and would call to let them know. She told me she was related to them. I think that Mr. Hunter is her uncle."

"Is her last name Franks?" Bobby asked, with a glare that could kill someone.

"Yes, it is. But what does that have to do with what happened here?"

"Did she talk to the Hunters?" Bobby asked.

"Yes," the attorney said. "But they couldn't meet us here, so I came out to tell Lieutenant Glen that they will be in my office later this afternoon."

The second ambulance pulled up to get Officer Franks. The EMTs put him in the back.

Bobby looked at one of the officers and said, "Follow this man back to his office, and get Mrs. Franks and bring her to the hospital. Don't tell her anything. And you, Mr. Attorney, you tell the Hunters we found two dead policemen here at their farm, and I will be by to see them as soon as I get there—and they better not leave."

"Lieutenant Glen was dead?" the attorney asked.

"Yes" Bobby said with a tear in his eye, hoping to himself that he was telling a lie.

***

Bobby got to the hospital and headed to emergency room looking for Lieutenant Glen. He asked the nurse at the desk where he was. She told him that they rushed Lieutenant Glen straight to surgery. Bobby said to the nurse, "Please, if anyone comes looking for information on Lieutenant Glen, tell them nothing. Tell them you don't even know him. Please—it is very important."

"OK, whatever you say. I'm too busy to answer any questions any-way," the nurse said, as she headed off to another emergency.

Mrs. Franks and the other officer walked into the emergency room. She wanted to know why she was here. Bobby walked over to her and said, "Did you tell your uncle that police officers were at the farm looking for them?"

"Yes, I did, and he wasn't happy about it. What is this all about?"

"Well, I believe he killed your husband and Lieutenant Glen."

"Jim is dead? No, he wouldn't do that!" She broke down in tears. "Where is my husband? I demand to know where he is. You're telling me a lie. You're a mean, cruel person. Who is your superior? I want to report you!" Mrs. Franks was hysterical.

"My superior is dead also, so you're out of luck. Take Mrs. Franks down to the morgue, and stay with her. No phone calls. You understand?" The attending officer shook his head, held Mrs. Franks's arm, and headed out of the waiting room. She was still yelling at Bobby, but he did not care.

A nurse handed Bobby a note. It was from the officer he had sitting with the man from the wreck. The note said, *Sergeant Carson, please come to the ICU.*

What now? he thought. He went to the ICU, and the officer told him to go in. "They're waiting for you. "Bobby walked in and saw the man from the wreck. The doctors had removed some of the bandages. The doctor asked Bobby, "Do you recognize this man now?"

Bobby couldn't believe his eyes. "That's Gary! Can he talk? Has he been conscious?"

"No," said the doctor, "but shouldn't be long. He's breathing on his own and is getting stronger, but I can't guarantee he'll remember anything."

"Please let me know when he can talk. And if you could let me know about my lieutenant? He's in surgery right now. Can you do that? I'm going to leave an officer outside until I know everyone is safe."

"As soon as I know anything, you will know," the doctor told Bobby.

Bobby left the hospital and headed to the attorney's office. By now, Bobby was at his wit's end. He called for backup to meet him there. He and the other officer walked into the attorney office. And there he was: Mr. Hunter, along with two thugs. Bobby told the officer, "Arrest all three of them."

"You can't do that," the attorney said. "You have no evidence on these men."

"Pull your legal crap down at the jail. Search these thugs good before you take them," Bobby told the young officer. "Let's get that car towed in also. Get hold of the officer at the hospital who is with Mrs. Franks, and have her arrested too. I'm tired of chasing my tail. I want all these ducks in one barrel." "But, Serge, Mrs. Franks just lost her husband. Are you sure you want to arrest her?" the officer with Bobby said.

"It's her fault he got killed, if my instincts are right. She tipped off the Hunters when we were there. We can sort all this out down at the jail. What do you think, Mr. Attorney?" Bobby was tired and fed up with everything.

The attorney looked at Mr. Hunter and said, "I will be there as soon as I can."

"You better have your butt down there when we get there if you want to get paid." Mr. Hunter wasn't happy about this outcome.

The attorney looked at Mr. Hunter and said, "I haven't seen a check in a while, so don't start threatening me now. I'll be there when I get there." It was obvious that the attorney was fed up with the Hunters too. With handcuffs on, out the door went Mr. Hunter and the two other men.

Bobby looked at the attorney and asked, "Have you seen Mrs. Hunter?"

"I saw her one time awhile back but not since. I got the impression she didn't want anything to do with whatever was going on," said the attorney.

With that, Bobby picked up one of the attorney's business cards and walked out the door. The card read, *Travis Trump, Attorney at Criminal Law.* We'll see, Bobby thought.

Chapter 10

THIS PLACE IS AMAZING

It was early November, and the weather was still not very cold, but of course where I had lived before, it would have been freezing by now. It was chilly, and I had to wear a coat, but it wasn't too bad.

The sun was just coming up, and everyone was eating breakfast and getting ready for school. I was getting homeschooled by Grandma, which was the best. After everyone left for school, I went out to the barn and helped feed the horses and muck out the stalls. Most people wouldn't like doing this, but to me being around here was the best place ever.

I was assigned two young colts to break to ride. Dad said this was the only way to see my talents. He said that Gary was right; I had good horse sense (whatever that meant, because I never thought Gary liked me). Dad talked a lot about Gary, but I never asked how he knew him. But I'm sure glad that Gary sent me here. After all my morning chores and work with the colts, Mom would take me to Grandma's house.

Grandma would have a little snack for me and my schoolwork all laid out on the kitchen table. Math was always my hardest subject, so Grandma had math first thing. She had a way of explaining things that no one else could. Before long, it was lunchtime.

Grandma came into the kitchen and checked my work and was pleased. "Today we are going to start something different," Grandma said.

"What, Grandma?" I loved it when Grandma would say this because it was always fun.

"Well, you are going to start cooking. It's time you learned how to feed yourself and to know where the food comes from," Grandma said.

"I know where the food comes from, Grandma. That sounds silly," I said. But, boy, was that the wrong thing to say. Grandma led Jim and me to the very back of her property, which I had no idea was there. She had a big greenhouse. It was magical. It had all kinds of plants and herbs, and the smells were awesome. "Grandma, I had no idea this was here; this is beautiful."

"I thought you knew where the food comes from, my friend?" Grandma said with a smile. Jim's nose was in the air, smelling all the smells. It was something.

"OK, Scout," Grandma started, "show me a tomato plant. What about a potato plant? What about rosemary, thyme? What about dill? Or maybe show me what you *can* identify?" Grandma said with a big grin. "Grandma, most of these are seedlings. How can you tell what they are?" I was looking around, still amazed at the smells. "I never knew you had all this."

"Where do you think I get my medicines that I make for people? I want you to learn what these things can do for you. I know you like to eat, but you need to know what can make you well, what can make you strong." Grandma was serious now.

"Can we make that soup you gave me that night I was hurt? That soup was incredible. I dream about that soup." My mouth was watering.

"One day. But that was medicine to make you stronger, and it all comes from here. Now, let's learn some of these plants." Grandma showed me some of the plants and told me about what they could do. It was overwhelming for me, but it was interesting.

Then we went into another part of the greenhouse where there were all kinds of flowers. "This is beautiful, Grandma."

"Scout, flowers are pretty, but they have healing powers also. They are here for many reasons, not just to smell nice and look pretty. You have a lot to learn."

"And I thought math was hard."

"You have no idea, my little friend," Grandma said with that smile of hers that I could feel deep in my soul. As we walked back through the greenhouse, Grandma picked some flowers and then a little of this and that and put it all in a small basket.

"What are we going to do with all of this? Are we going to make center planter for the table?" I asked.

Grandma looked at me with a little disappointment. "This is lunch, my dear. Now, come on. It's your turn to cook lunch. We have company coming."

Fear took over. "You want *me* to cook lunch? I can't even boil water without burning it." I was in a panic now.

"No time like the present to learn. Now, come on. We have a lot to do." And off to the house we went. At least Jim was excited; he was jumping around and wagging his tail, like all this was for him.

We returned to the house, and Grandma laid all these things on the table, and she started telling me what this does for you and how to fix this and add that. We had a pot on the stove and a pan to go in the oven. She had blooms from a flower that she stuffed with herbs and laid on the pan, and she had me put other herbs and green things in the pot, with some salt and pepper. Grandma explained what each thing was. And there was no meat, just beautiful plants. The smells were awesome. I couldn't believe that we could eat these things.

It wasn't long before she was setting dishes on the table. She put four settings out. She made some kind of tea with some of the things we got from the greenhouse. She put ice in the glasses.

There was a knock at the door. I opened it and saw Mom and Dad. I thought, Oh great, I get to poison the two people who care about me.

"Hi, Scout. We hear you're cooking lunch," Mom said with a smile.

Dad didn't look as excited. "I hope we live through this," he said with a wink.

"Me too," I said, but I was serious.

Grandma said, "Put some soup in the bowls, Scout." And then Grandma pulled out those poor flowers she put in the oven and put them on a plate.

Everything smell great. I couldn't believe all this came out of that greenhouse. We sat down, Grandma blessed the plants and the spirits that gave her the knowledge to fix this, and we started eating. It was one of the best meals I'd ever had. It warmed my heart, like that soup Grandma had made me before. Mom and Dad loved it, and that was the best part. They told me how good it was and left. I washed the dishes and went back to my lessons with a happy belly.

∗∗∗

That afternoon, I was sitting on the dock, watching the dolphins playing in the creek. The tide had just started going out. There must have been six or seven dolphins, and I loved watching them. They came by every afternoon. Maybe they were always there...I didn't know. But every time I sat on the dock, they were there.

"What are you doing, Scout?" Tommy walked up, looking at me.

"Just watching the dolphins. How was school today? Anything new going on?" I asked these questions, but Tommy wasn't paying any attention. He was looking at the dolphins, and by now there were quite a few more. They looked really restless. After a few minutes, Tommy yelled at Frankie, "Get the life vest! Meet me at the boat! Come on, Scout. You're going to like this. Come on!"

Tommy was so excited. It was contagious. I don't know why, but I was just as excited. While running to little John's boat, Frankie came running with three life vests.

"What about John and Mike?" I asked.

"It's their night to feed horses," Tommy replied as he pushed the boat in the water.

"Where are we going?" I asked while we put on the life jackets. Tommy pulled the cord to start the motor. Birds were flying down the creek in the direction the dolphins were going. There was so much excitement between Tommy, Frankie, the birds, the dolphins–it was crazy.

Finally, we stopped. The dolphins were swimming in circles, slapping their tails. It had to have been twenty-five to thirty dolphins. Birds of all types were sitting on the bank. All but me seemed to know what was about to happen.

"Tommy?" I was fixing to say something when suddenly a group of the dolphins raced toward the bank. Fish came flying out of the water, the dolphins right behind them. The dolphins swam up on the bank and got a mouthful of fish. The birds joined in. It was like a celebration of some sort. It was very exciting. Everything was working together. Tommy and Frankie sat and watched, as if it were the first time that they had seen this. Then, as fast as it had happened, it was over. Tommy started the boat again, and we headed back home, never saying a word. I wanted to remember this–every amazing detail.

We came home, put the boat up, and walked to the house. I wanted to talk about what had happened. No one said a word until we got to the house and Mom asked, "Where did you all go in such a hurry?"

"The dolphins were feeding on the bank, so we took Scout to see it. I love watching them when they do this." Franking was grinning from ear to ear.

"It was amazing," I said.

"If people could learn to share like the dolphins do, this would be a better world. Animals are amazing; I never get tired of how they help each other and help us," Tommy said.

John and Mike walked into the house. "What's going on?" Mike asked.

We all went into the kitchen and talked about the day while Mom started cooking dinner. There were no secrets in this house. There was no anger in this house. I never knew there was a place or people like this—and they made me part of it. I never wanted to leave. Jim and all the other dogs were laid out on the floor and looked just has happy as everyone else.

Grandma came walking into the kitchen with some things to eat for dinner. All the food was ready, and we sat, ate, and talked. "Thanksgiving is around the corner. Does anyone here have any ideas on what they want to have?" Grandma asked.

"I want gumbo," Frankie said.

"What's gumbo?" I asked.

"It's better than anything you will have to eat," Frankie said.

"I haven't had anything that wasn't good since I've been here," I said.

"OK," Grandma started, "let's have a vote. Who wants gumbo for Thanksgiving?" There was a big "Yes!" from everyone. "Well, gumbo it is." I had never even heard of gumbo, but if Grandma cooked it, it would have to be good. This was the first time I had ever looked forward to Thanksgiving.

After we had eaten and washed the dishes (and, by the way, we never stopped talking), Grandma gathered up her things and was heading toward the door. The phone rang. I had never heard the phone ring or even noticed it on the wall. No one had a cell phone here, and I hadn't noticed till now. The phone continued ringing. I had chills going down my spine. Grandma stopped in her tracks as Mom answered the phone.

"Hello," Mom said and then listened. It seemed like a long time before she said, "When?" There was another long pause. "How are you?" Mom asked. "OK. Yes, she is fine...OK. Get well. All is good here...OK. See you soon...Bye." With that, Mom hung up the phone.

I didn't realize I had been holding my breath. "Breathe, girl" Grandma said, as she put her hand on my back. I exhaled. I hadn't felt this scared since I left. I had put all of those bad memories behind me.

Willy popped into my head—all bloody, lying on the ground.

Tears were flowing down my face, and before I knew it, I couldn't stop crying. I was curled up on the floor. Jim was sitting next to me.

Grandma and Mom both were trying to console me, but it wasn't working. I got up, ran to my room, and slammed the door. Jim barely made it in. I crawled up on the bed and cried.

Mom tried to come in, but Grandma stopped her. "Give her a minute or two," Grandma said. "She needs to remember. She has to face the demons."

"Not alone she doesn't." Mom was mad.

"She's not alone." Grandma had such a calming voice. "She knows that, but some things you have to face by yourself. Maybe after this she will talk about what happened, and we can help her though it." Mom and Grandma went back into the kitchen and started talking. I could hear them but wasn't able to understand what they were saying. After a few minutes, there was a knock on the door, and the door cracked open.

"Can I come in?" a little voice said. It was Frankie. No one can say no to Frankie. I nodded my head, and he came in. In his typical Frankie way, he didn't say a word and just crawled up into the bed with me and Jim. I still couldn't stop crying, but it was nice having Jim and little Frankie with me.

"Who was that on the phone?" Dad asked.

"It was Gary." Mom said. "He had been in an accident and is in the hospital. They said he would be there for a while, but they are expecting a full recovery. Then he asked about Scout. He said that they may be coming for her soon but didn't know when." Mom was really sad.

"We will do everything we can for Scout. Don't worry," Dad said.

Grandma walked out the door and began heading home. I followed her out and asked, "Can I go with you, Grandma?"

"Sure, dear. Come on." We walked to Grandma's house in silence. That's why I loved being around her; she didn't ask a lot of questions. Jim was running around, happy to be out, even though a cold wind was blowing.

***

By the time we got to Grandma's house, we were freezing, and it started raining. Grandma walked into the house and started a fire to warm us up, and that was the only light in the house.

Grandma went into the other room and came out with heavy jackets. "Come on, girl. We are going outside."

"In the rain? Really?" I asked.

"I want to show you something. Are you OK?" Grandma was smiling.

"Yes. I'm sorry for all that. I don't know what happened. Are you all going to send me back there?" I felt tears coming to my eyes again.

"Come on, Scout. Let's see if we can feel stronger before continuing this conversation." And with that, out into the rain we went. It started thundering and lightning. All those memories came flooding back. The rain hid the tears.

We walked till we came to a clearing. There was a tarp over what looked like a pit. There was one more bright lightning flash and clap of thunder, and then Grandma uncovered the pit.

The rain stopped. Grandma started a huge fire. The blaze was twice as high as I've ever seen flames go. Grandma picked up these drums that, when she tapped on them, gave a sound so different from any I'd ever heard before. The flames in the fire were a multitude of colors. They danced around with the rhythm of the drum. Grandma started to chant. I'd never heard anything like it. Her eyes did not seem to be hers. The flames spoke to her. I sat back and looked at them, in awe. Never have I seen fire act like this. The flames were becoming people.They were my real mom and dad, and there were my real brothers. I hadn't thought about them since I'd been here. They weren't a good sight. Then there I was, standing by them. I could see the bruises on my face and my brothers, with that hateful look they had. Then there were my parents, with no care for me whatsoever. And then there was Willy, standing in the distance. I knew then why Grandma brought me here.

After a while, we headed back to the house. It didn't seem like we were out there that long, but when we got back, the sun was starting to rise. "Grandma, I know I have to go back, but I don't want to. What am I going to do?" I was feeling a little better.

"We don't know when you have to go back, but we will try our best to bring you back here if that is what you want." Grandma was always honest.

"Grandma, did you see anything in that fire? How long were we out there?"

"We were out there long enough. And yes, I saw what you saw—and more. I know what happened and why you are here. I'm sorry what you've been through; it is really sad. This is your real family. We love you and will do anything we can to get you back here. But yes, you'll have to go back when they say. We have to do this the right way. Do you understand, Scout?"

"I know, but I'm scared."

"Go take a hot bath, and take a nap for a while. I'll fix you something to eat." Grandma walked off toward the kitchen.

After my bath, I put on a large t-shirt laid out for me. I felt relieved for some reason. I felt clean inside and out. I lay down on the bed with Jim beside me. I got under the covers, and that was the last thought I had.

When I woke, it was dark. I could hear people talking in the other room. I got up and dressed. My clothes were on the bed, cleaned and folded. I walked into the other room, in the dark of course. It had become a habit not to turn on any lights; I liked the dark. As I got close to the room, I could see the glow of the fire in the fireplace. The food smell was making me want to be in a hurry. When I walked into the room, Frankie was the first to run up to me. "Are you all right?" he said to me.

"Yes, I'm good. Thank you, Frankie. You have to be the sweetest person I've ever known."

"Thanks a lot, Scout."

"What about us?" Tommy, Mike, and John said at the same time.

"I love everyone in this room," I said, not realizing I had a big grin on my face. I really did love everyone in this room.

Mom spoke. "Scout, that was Gary on the phone. He said you may have to go back soon. But it will be after Thanksgiving; I'll make sure of that. I just found out your birthday is coming up. Were you not going to tell us?"

"I don't know. I really hadn't thought about it. It was never a day that anyone ever cared about."

"Well, it will be a special day here," Dad said. And with that, we sat down and ate and talked and laughed. What a great night.

***

Later, Tommy, John, Mike, Frankie, and I walked home in the dark. There wasn't a moon in the sky, but there must have been a million stars to light the way.

"What do you want for your birthday?" Tommy asked me, with a grin.

"What's that grin all about, Tommy? You aren't going to do anything weird, are you?" I was a little worried. I loved these guys, but you never knew.

"Come on, Scout. It's going to be your birthday. What do you want? Or what would you like to do? It'll be *your* day."

Tommy looked sincere.

"Yeah, come on, Scout. What do you want to do? This will be the best day ever." Frankie was jumping up and down and couldn't be still. That little boy's smile could light up a hurricane.

"I don't know. I never had a birthday party. I'd like to go on a trail ride and just hang out with the horses. Would that be OK?" I didn't know what to ask for, but I knew I wanted to do that.

"That would be great! John and I will take care of the rest of the day," Mike said.

"What about me? What do I do?" Frankie said, looking a little left out.

"I was hoping you'd go with me on my trail ride, Frankie." I had to say something, and I'd love little Frankie coming along.

"Really?"

"Yes, Frankie. I'd love it if everyone was there. It would be fun just to hang out before I have to go back. So, that's what I want for my birthday. Please?"

"When is your birthday? I mean, the date?" John asked.

"It's the eighteenth" I said.

"Saturday? Boy, we're going to have the best birthday ever," Tommy said.

The rest of the walk was pretty quiet. We just looked at the stars and walked arm in arm. I was really going to miss these boys, and I already knew that these would always be the best days of my life. And then, out of nowhere, it started raining. I mean raining. It came pouring down. It turned this nice fifty-degree night into a cold, wet forty-degree night. We started running to the house, but it was still a good ways off.

We run till we gave out. Little Frankie was having a hard time keeping up. So we started back, walking and laughing. We were soaked to the bone, but it took away the thoughts about having to leave. When we got back, Mom was at the door with towels and hot chocolate.

We dried off and put on dry clothes. By then, we were ready for another cup of hot chocolate. Mom, Dad, and everyone went out on the porch to watch the rain. No one said much, but all I could think about was, This is where it all started, on the front porch. One day, I'd have a porch like this. If everyone had a front porch like this, no one would get angry. They would rock their anger away while the dolphins sing. No one would stay mad long. After a while, I looked around, and everyone had gone inside. I was all alone with my thoughts. And that was OK too.

Chapter 11

LIEUTENANT GLEN (ADAM)

Back at the hospital, Bobby was talking to Lieutenant Glen about the Hunters being arrested when Nancy and Vic came walking through the door.

"That's enough. The nurses said you've been in here long enough. You need to get some rest too, Sergeant Carson. You look like hell," said Nancy. "Adam, I know you need your rest. So—downtime. Vic wanted to see you about something. I can't figure out what he's talking about." Nancy looked a little on edge.

"The trial is the first of December. We have to be ready," Bobby said.

"I'm glad to see Adam doing so well and can't believe he is," Nancy began. "He almost died, you know. The doctors didn't think he would live. Now that he *is* going to live, I won't let *you* kill him. Now go get some rest. *I* need rest. *Adam* needs rest. And this boy needs to get something off his mind so *he* can rest. And then I have to go home to my daughter, who thinks she's my mother. And it's driving me crazy. So please, let's just get this moment in time over with." Nancy was definitely frazzled.

Bobby was walking out the door when Lieutenant Glen said, "You may want to hear this. It may be important." Bobby turned around and sat down.

"Well, *I* don't want to know," Nancy said, "so I'll go get a cup of coffee and just chill for a few minutes. But that's it; you have to get some rest. I feel like a robot saying the same thing over and over. I'll be back." Nancy walked off thinking to herself, I can't believe I just said that. Then she giggled a little to herself, got a cup of coffee, sat down, and watched all the people in the hospital run here and there.

"What in the world was that all about?" Lieutenant Glen looked at Vic for some sort of answer, an explanation of Nancy's outburst, but Vic was just staring off into space like nothing in the world was happening at that moment. Bobby looked as puzzled as Lieutenant Glen.

"OK, Vic what's going on?" Lieutenant Glen started.

Vic moved his head around, looked at him, and said, "Adam, I'm glad you didn't die."

"Thank you, Vic. I'm glad I didn't die too. Now what's going on that you need to talk to me about?"

Vic looked at Bobby and said, "Your wife is sick. She needs to go to the doctor."

Bobby looked confused. But after the last session with Vic, he was listening. "How do you know?" Bobby asked, knowing his wife had been looking a little weak lately.

"Is that what you had to say, Vic? Is that what this is about?" Lieutenant Glen looked at Bobby with great concern.

"No, there is a lady who is hurt real bad, and she is trapped. I see her mostly at night. She is very weak. I think you need to go find her," Vic said in a very positive tone.

"Where is she, Vic? Can you describe where she is?" Lieutenant Glen was very concerned with what Vic was saying.

"There are a lot of trees and old buildings. She was crying a lot, but now she just sits." Vic was staring into space, as if he was there with that person.

"How long have you been seeing her, Vic?" Lieutenant Glen asked, knowing time meant nothing to this boy.

"Don't know, Adam," Vic replied.

"Do you know her name?" Names meant nothing to Vic either.

"No, Adam. But she needs help. Are you going to help her?"

"Yes, Vic, but we need more information. OK. Let's try this: What kind of buildings? What do they look like?" Lieutenant Glen was getting tired.

"The kind of buildings that animals live in. But no animals live in it now. It is very old."

"Good, Vic. Now, how many buildings are there?" Lieutenant Glen continued.

"Just one big one and one little one. She is in the little one. Big trees all around it. That is all I know. I want to go now."

Nancy walked into the room. "Has everyone had enough fun?"

Vic got up and said, "I want to go home now."

"Come on, Vic. Let's go. And, Sergeant Carson, would you walk me to my car? Adam, get some rest. See you tomorrow."

Nancy walked out of the room, and everyone else followed. Lieutenant Glen just smiled and said to himself, "That's my sister. And she wonders where Mary Beth gets her attitude from." This made him laugh, which made him hurt really bad. His wounds were very severe, and they would take time to heal. With that, he sat back, picked up a book, and started reading.

He couldn't get Vic out of his head. Old buildings that animals stay in. Where would an old barn be? He knew most of the area; he grew up here. Big trees…big trees…Where? Or what kind? And Bobby's wife needed to see a doctor? What did all this have to do with anything? He was sure it does, but what? He leaned back into his pillow, and all his questions were gone. He was fast asleep.

Bobby came back to tell him he would call in the morning but saw it was no use. He was sound asleep. "Sleep well, my good friend," Bobby said to him softly, and he closed the door.

Bobby went to another room and opened the door to see Gary. Gary was sitting up in bed watching television. "Hi, Bobby. How are you?" Gary asked, just glad to see someone.

"I'm good. I hear you're getting out of here tomorrow. Do you know where you're going?"

"Yes. I got a room till after court, then I'm going back home. I'd like to go home before the court date, if that is OK? Just for a few days." Gary tried to feel out Bobby to see where he stood on all this.

"We'll see," Bobby said. "But in the meantime, do you recall any old building that animals live in with big trees around it?" Bobby said out of the blue.

Gary looked at him strange. "What are you talking about?"

"Well, we got a strange tip about a lady being held in an old building. I'm thinking it may be an old barn. But there are two buildings: one big, one small. There may be some large trees grown around them, so they wouldn't be easy to see. Does this sound like any place you might have seen?" Bobby was trying to explain this the best he could. He remembered how crazy he thought Lieutenant Glen was the first time he met Vic.

"You know, this might sound crazy, but when I came to...They knocked me in the head, you know. Man, that hurt and still does. But anyway, when I came to, we were in some musty smelling place. I remember because it was hard to breathe. They had a blindfold on me. I couldn't see where we were, and we weren't there long. I was in and out of it for a while, so time-wise I have no idea. Could have been an hour or we were there or days. I was pretty loopy." Gary was trying hard to remember.

"Were they holding anyone else besides you?" Bobby asked.

"I thought I heard moaning, but like I said, I was in and out of it, so I'm not sure what was real and wasn't." Gary was trying; Bobby could tell.

Bobby reached over and gave Gary his card with his cell phone number on the back. "Call me if you need a ride tomorrow or if you can think of anything else. Focus on that musty, old-building smell.

I'm going to the house. Have a good night. We'll talk soon." Bobby got up and walked out the door.

Gary thought it strange for Bobby to just stop talking and leave like that. But whatever. He would talk to him tomorrow.

Bobby got to his car and called his wife. She answered, "Hello, Bobby. When are you coming home so I can have you something to eat."

"I'm on my way now; just leaving the hospital. You feeling OK?" Bobby asked.

"Yes, fine. Why do you ask? Are *you* OK?" she asked.

"Yes, fine. I'm on my way home. See you soon. Love you. Bye." Bobby hung up the phone, almost in tears. It had been a long, stressful five weeks. He would be glad to be home and see his family, and he hoped Vic was wrong. Was Vic ever wrong? he thought.

Tomorrow was the bond hearing for Mr. Hunter and his merry followers. Bobby had a lot on his mind when he got home, but everything there seemed good. He had his dinner and fell asleep as his head hit his pillow. Next to him, Sue just looked at him and smiled at the man she loved so much.

Chapter 12

JESSIE

When Bobby woke the next morning, the first thing that came to mind was Jessie. Jessie might know some old farms around here. He grew up right here, and so did his family.

Bobby took a shower and was dressed in minutes. He went into the kitchen and saw Carol and Sue eating breakfast. He walked over, kissed Carol on the head, gave Sue a kiss, grabbed some toast, and headed out the door. He turned around and said, "Love you both. And, Sue, let me know if you don't feel well. Hope to be home early. Love you both." Out the door he went.

Carol looked at her Mom. "Are you OK?"

"As far as I know, sweetie. Your dad has been acting weird lately."

Bobby pulled out his phone and called Jessie. No answer. But he could leave a message. It had been weeks since he had talked to or even seen Jessie. Bobby drove by the house where Jessie lived, but no one was there. The people next door said they had moved or gone on vacation because they hadn't seen them in a while.

He went by where the horses were being taken care of. Someone else was feeding the horses. Bobby got out of the truck, walked over to the young man feeding the animals, and asked him, "Where is Jessie?"

"Lieutenant Glen asked me to help Jessie out. He might be here later. I'm not sure. How is Lieutenant Glen doing? I heard he got shot up pretty bad," the young boy said.

"What is your name, son, and how do you know Lieutenant Glen?" Bobby asked, not sure who this kid was.

"My name's Tony Duncan. I've known Lieutenant Glen—or Adam, as I call him—all my life. He and my dad are best friends, and he knew I liked horses and asked me to help out."

"Well, nice to meet you. My name is Bobby Carson." They shook hands. "Have you seen Jessie lately, Tony?"

"He comes around about once a day, usually in the early evenings," Tony said. "If you see him today, please tell him to call me. Here is my card." Bobby handed Tony his card. Tony nodded his head, and Bobby got in his car and headed to the station. Time to go to work.

While driving to the station, his phone rang. Bobby looked and saw that it was Jessie. "Where are you? And are you OK?" Bobby was very concerned.

"I'm fine. Lieutenant Glen told me to stay out of sight for a while, till I heard from him. But then I saw that he got shot, and I wasn't sure what to do. When I saw you called, I thought maybe you knew something." Jessie was just rambling on.

"Can I see you today around lunchtime to talk? Mr. Hunter and his crew have a bond hearing in the morning, and I would like to ask you some questions if that is OK." There was more Bobby wanted to talk about, but that was a start. He was just glad Jessie was OK.

"Sure, Bobby. What about that hamburger place on Main Street? Big Boys I think it's called. And can Mae come? She loves those hamburgers from that place." Jessie sounded hungry.

"Yes, please bring Mae. Love to see you both. I'll see you there at eleven thirty if that suits you," Bobby replied.

"See you then, Bobby." And Jessie hung up.

Bobby got to the office, sat down, and went through all the paperwork on his desk. He talked to a few of his officers to discuss a few ongoing cases, and, before he knew it, it was eleven o'clock. He got in his car and headed to the restaurant. Jessie and Mae were already there. They were waiting in their car. Bobby walked over to them, and then they all walked into the restaurant together.

"Is Lieutenant Glen going to be OK, Bobby?" Jessie started the conversation.

"Yes, he will make a good recovery, but he is going to have some bad scars. It will take some time before he will be back to work—if he comes back. I think, if I where him, I'd take a long time off." Bobby looked at Mae and said, "How are you, Miss Mae? I hope you're well. You look beautiful." He blushed a little. Her beauty had caught him off guard. There was so much going on. He guessed he hadn't stopped to look.

"Why, thank you, Sergeant Carson. *You* look like hell. You need to get some rest. Sorry...I shouldn't have said all that. Have you heard from Scout? Is she OK? When will she be coming back? Is she coming back?" Mae was on a roll.

Jessie stopped her and said, "Let's just hear what he has to say, and then we'll ask questions. OK, Mae?" Mae sat back patiently to hear what Bobby had to say.

The waitress walked up and said, "Can I take your order, please?"

Jessie said, "Cheeseburger and fries with sweet tea, please."

"Same here," Bobby said.And Mae nodded her head as if to say "Me too."

"Boy, I wish all my orders were this easy," the waitress said as she walked away.

"Are we safe now, Bobby? Is all this mess over with now that you have the Hunters?" Jessie was tired of all this drama and hiding.

"I don't know for sure. I want you to stay where you are. I don't want to know where you are staying. I'm assuming Lieutenant Glen found you something and knows where you are. Just leave it at that. What I really want to talk to you about is, Do you know of any old, abandoned barns around here? I mean, old ones that have grown over with trees." Bobby couldn't wait any longer.

"What does that have to do with anything, Bobby?" Jessie looked confused.

"We have Mr. Hunter, but no one has seen or heard from Mrs. Hunter. We got kind of a weird tip that she was being held in an old barn with big trees all around it. I don't know if it's a good tip, but it's better than nothing. And I figured, since you grew up around here, you might have seen a place like this. Mr. Hunter is not talking. I just have a hunch she is still alive." Bobby almost sounded as though he was pleading.

"Jessie, remember that place near your daddy's house?" Mae asked. "He said it was an old sharecropper place...had some old house and an outbuilding...could have been a barn. That place would be gone by now. It was old and run down when we were young-ins. Your daddy told us he would beat our behinds if he ever caught us there. Do you remember, Jessie? Up there on Red House Road?"

Jessie looked at Mae and said, "You think it's still there? It's been awhile, but it looked like it was falling down then."

The food came to the table, and Bobby said, "Do you think you can still find this place? We are running out of time if this lady is still alive."

Jessie called the waitress over and asked, "Could you put these iced teas in to-go cups and bring our bill? We need to go somewhere. Thank you."

By the time she came back with the bill and the teas, everyone had eaten their hamburgers and were ready to go. Bobby paid the bill and left the tip. Jessie tried but Bobby insisted.

"Let's go in my car," Bobby said. "We can ride together and catch up on a few things." They all got into Bobby's unmarked police car. Jessie laughed as they got in.

Bobby said, "What are you laughing at, Jessie?"

"I don't know why you think that just because you don't write *police car* on the side that people don't know that this is a police car,"

Jessie said, grinning. "Now, two Black people getting in—we look like we just got arrested."

"Yeah. And he let us bring our sweet tea with us. Now *that* is the way to be arrested," Mae added to Jessie's remark. "*Now* can I have some questions answered? I think I've been patient long enough." Mae got serious. "Where is my Scout, and is she all right?"

"Turn right up here, Bobby," Jessie said, giving directions.

"She's fine. Gary called the other day, and everything was good," Bobby answered, the best he could. All he had to go on was what Gary told him.

"When can we see her, and when will she be back? I bet she has grown a foot since she left," said Mae.

"I'm not sure, Mae. But if we wrap this case up and put that Hunter man in jail, maybe we could all get our lives back to normal—whatever that is." Bobby was doing the best he could.

"Take the next right, up here. It's been a long time since I've been up in these parts. OK. Right up here on the left should be close to where that old place was. We'll have to hike through the woods to find it. It looks like some cars have been parking here. That's odd because there's nothing around here." Jessie looked around.

"Are you sure this is it, Jessie?" Mae asked.

Jessie nodded his head, and Bobby said, "Let's check it out. Mae, I want you to stay with the car." He showed Mae how to use the radio if needed. Then Bobby called dispatch to let them know his location and if Mae called, to send the cavalry.

Jessie and Bobby started walking through the woods. "Looks as though there's a path here," Jessie said. "It hasn't been used much, but it's a path."

Bobby pulled Jessie back and stopped dead still. Bobby whispered, "Do you hear that? I hear somebody talking." Jessie nodded his head; he could hear it too. "Jessie, can you shoot a gun?" Jessie nodded yes but didn't like the idea of using one under these circumstances. Bobby handed Jessie a gun and whispered, "If things go wrong, get back to the car. Use this to protect yourself, and get out of here. You understand?"

"Yes," Jessie said, feeling sick. This wasn't what he had planned for today.

They started walking to where they heard the voices. As they got closer, Bobby recognized one of the voices. He looked at Jessie and whispered, "Go back to the car, and call for backup."

"I'm not leaving you," Jessie said, with all the courage he could muster up.

"Yes, you are. I need help, and if this goes bad, you need to be there for Mae. Now go."

Bobby knew Jessie didn't need to be there. Jessie headed back toward the car as quietly as he could.

Bobby walked closer to the voices to confirm his suspicions. As he looked toward where the voices were coming from, he saw these huge trees. How did Vic do that? It's amazing, Bobby thought. The voices were getting louder and clearer. The best he could tell at the moment, there were two men. One of them sounded just like that lawyer the Hunters used.

"What are we going to do with her?" one of the men was saying. Bobby was being as still as he could and out of sight. He wanted to know what he was dealing with and how many men there were.

Then the second voice said, "I don't want anything to do with this crap. I didn't sign up for this. All I want is the money owed to me. Mr. Hunter can find someone else to represent him in court. I'm done." Bobby thought, That's him. Oh damn. What's his name?

He was trying to figure out what that man's name was when he heard another voice: "You aren't going anywhere, lawyer boy. You've already seen the lady, and so if you aren't going to play with us, we can't let you go anywhere."

So now there were three. The odds weren't good.

Bobby weighed his options. He wondered if the lady was still alive. And was the lady Mrs. Hunter? He felt sure it was. He hoped

Jessie got back to the car and called for help. In the meantime, he just sat and listened.

The voices of the three men went back and forth. Travis Trump—that was that lawyer's name. He sounded like he was fixing to get his ass trumped. Bobby couldn't believe he couldn't remember his name.

"Well, I have a plan," said one of the voices. "Joe, we could kill these two and get our asses out of here—because we really don't have a dog in this fight. We were hired just to watch this lady; now everyone is in jail. All I'm saying: get rid of these two and get our happy asses out of here. These two are the only ones who know who we are." The man did have a point. No one knew anyone else was involved in this till now. Bobby tried to think of some kind of distraction. At least he knew that the woman was still alive. He was thinking about Jessie. He would be getting to the car about now, and it would take about fifteen to twenty minutes before backup arrived.

The conversation was starting to get really heated. That lawyer was just wanting to get killed. While they were arguing, Bobby decided it was a good time to move in closer. He really wanted to get a good look at these guys. As he was crawling through the undergrowth, he heard something behind him. He froze. Then he heard a whisper and looked, and it was Jessie.

"Help is coming," Jessie whispered.

"Stay here, and watch out for me. I'm going to try and get a better look," Bobby whispered back.

Jessie got behind a tree and could hear these guys at each other's throats. He hoped Bobby knew what he was doing because they sounded like they really wanted to kill someone or each other. Jessie wasn't sure which but didn't care as long as it wasn't him or Bobby. I'm starting to like the guy, Jessie thought while watching Bobby crawl through the woods.

Then it started raining. It was a cold, steady rain. It didn't take long for Bobby to be soaked. He never wore the right clothes or had his jacket when he needed it. The good thing was everyone who was arguing had gone inside the old shack. This could be good or bad, but it gave Bobby an opportunity to get close. He was looking through the window when he saw one of the men put a gun to Travis Trump's head. Well, it was now or never. That boy was going to be killed. Bobby was fixing to tap on the window when he saw police coming through the trees. They surrounded the shack and stormed in. It was over. The two guys with guns gave up pretty easily, but Travis Trump wouldn't shut up. Mrs. Hunter was tied up on a bed. She didn't look well.

"Call for an ambulance for this lady," Bobby told one of his officers while he untied her. "Are you OK?" he asked her softly.

"I don't know…I don't know" was all she could say.

Jessie walked in after he saw the bad guys come out in handcuffs. "Boy, that lawyer man doesn't like handcuffs, and he won't shut up. How is Mrs. Hunter?" Jessie looked at the lady.

"Oh, Jessie. Is that you? Please be Jessie." She sat up and wrapped her arms around him. "Are you OK. Is Mae OK?"

"They said that they had killed you and Mae. It broke my heart. I couldn't stand the thought." Mrs. Hunter was sobbing uncontrollably.

"We're fine, Mrs. Hunter. Everyone is fine," Jessie assured her.

"What about poor Gary? They beat him till he couldn't move and took him away. Did you find his body?" Now she was hysterical.

"He's fine too, ma'am."

She let go of Jessie because of pure exhaustion. When she lay back down, the EMT was there to get her.

"She's been through a lot," Bobby said to Jessie.

"How did you know she was here, Bobby?" Jessie replied.

"Long story, Jessie. I'll tell you about it another day."

This day was done. Mrs. Hunter said she would testify against her husband and all that he did. Mr. Hunter and crew wouldn't get out on bond and would spend a long time in jail for insurance fraud, murder, and kidnapping. That was just the short list.

Bobby came home feeling like the day was complete. He walked into the house, and his daughter ran to greet him. "Where is your mom, sweetie?" Bobby asked.

"She's in bed. She said she isn't feeling well."

Chapter 13

BIRTHDAY

It is a foggy, chilly morning. The clouds hung low, and you couldn't see a thing looking out the window from the kitchen. Mom had breakfast ready and waiting. Tommy walked into the kitchen and wandered over to the table to eat. "I can't believe Scout isn't up yet," Tommy said, sleepy-eyed.

"Well, to tell you the truth, my dear Tommy, everyone is out in the barn with horses saddled waiting on you," Mom said with a big grin.

"You're kidding me. No way!" Tommy jumped up and ran toward the door. Mom handed him a bacon-and-egg sandwich and said, "I think they even have *your* horse saddled." Tommy wasn't used to being the last one to the rodeo (so to speak).

John looked up as Tommy stumbled through the barn door. "I hope this little guy is who you were wanting to take. He's saddled and ready." John was holding a pretty bay colt, with a little white spot on his head. And that was all the white he had on him. Tommy had been riding him a good bit lately.

"Thank you, John. He'll be fine. He needs to go out in the open and see what he can do. It'll be good for him. Thanks," Tommy said, knowing John was being a smart-ass.

Mike, with a smirk, said, "Glad you got here before we left. We were fixing to leave you."

Tommy looked around for Scout and saw her in the back of the barn saddling up a little buckskin filly that she had been breaking to ride. Tommy walked over to her. "Do you think she's ready for this ride? It's awfully foggy out there this morning." Tommy sounded concerned about my little filly.

I liked this horse. I looked at Tommy and said, "She's very ready. She's one of the smartest young horses I've ever been on. And Jim will agree." Jim was sitting beside me, wagging his tail.

Everyone was putting their lunches in their saddle bags when Tommy realized he didn't get his lunch. Mike stopped him and said, "We put yours in your saddle bag–since you needed your beauty sleep this morning."

Tommy just smiled and said, "Thank you, Mike. So you're saying I'm looking good this morning?"

Everyone laughed and walked out of the barn with their horses. Frankie was the last one out the barn, with his pretty, little paint horse, who he named CJ. CJ was a seven-year-old brown and white paint gelding about fourteen hands tall–just right for Frankie. He loved that little horse. We all got on our horses and rode out into the fog. Through the kitchen window, Mom watched as much as she could through the fog. In this somber moment, she saw those five figures vanish into the fog.

We put Frankie in front since he had the most broke horse of all of them. Mike was riding a young black filly. He had been riding her a lot in the woods lately, and things didn't seem to bother her at all. John's little sorrel filly wasn't too happy with this outing at the moment. She was jumping this way and that way.

"You want to go back and get another horse, John?" Tommy said, looking a little worried.

"No. She'll be OK. Just give her some time," Mike chimed in. Mike was a really good hand around horses. If he thought it was all good, you could believe him.

Soon, everyone was riding along happily. The sun was starting to poke through the damp fog. We were all just as wet as if we had gone swimming. But now the sun was coming through, and you could already feel the warmth from it.

"Scout, where do you want to go?" Frankie asked.

"Let's go down to the creek, where the dolphins like to eat. I figure that by the time we get to the inlet, the tide will be low, so we can cross without any problems. This way we can ride all the way on the beach once we get to the beach. We can come back down the sand roads coming home." I had all this figured out.

"Wow, Scout! You've turned into a real islander. Checked up on the tides and everything. Nice planning," Mike said.

"Well, I didn't want to screw up my first real birthday," I said, with a smile on my face.

"Going down to the beach is a long way to get where you want to go," Tommy said.

"Yeah, but I've never ridden a horse on the beach before, and it sounded like fun. Plus Grandma said it was the best way to go. She also told me when the tide would be right and the path home. I can't take any credit on this one. I tried," I said.

We got to the beach, and the sky was almost clear. The fog was gone, and the water was smooth. No waves at all; it looked like a lake. We got to the water's edge and galloped down it, Frankie in the lead. Frankie's little horse, CJ, never missed a trick. He just galloped along, like it was what he did every day. Now, John's little horse was a whole other story. That little horse didn't like anything: she did not like the sand, she did not like the water, she did not want to gallop. What she did want was to buck John off and go back home. We all started to slow down when John said, "Keep going. She'll get tired soon. Just keep going." John was waving his hands. "Go on." By the time we got to the inlet, John's horse had subsided, going along with the plan. But at the inlet, John's horse didn't like this change in plan.

An inlet is a wide spot on the beach where water flows inland at high tide. And at low tide, it's still there but not as deep and with not as much current. Now, Frankie's horse, CJ, just walked through, like there was nothing to it. My little buckskin filly went through fairly well; she was a little skittish but OK. Tommy and Mike did fine also. But poor John. His horse came across there like a jackrabbit. She would leap straight up in the air, all four feet out of the water, and come down splashing. It was a good thing the inlet wasn't very wide at low tide—about two leaps and she was across.

"Now that was fun," John said, with a big ole grin on his face. We all laughed and headed into the grove of big, old oak trees. We could have gone down the beach, but there was a lot of driftwood that way, and we figured John's horse had seen all it needed to today. She was used to being in the woods. The sun was good and warm now. There was a breeze coming from the beach that was nice. The air was still a little chilly but nice.

We came to a clearing at the main creek that circles the island. There was a big barrel there that catches rainwater, so we could water the horses. Grandma checked it yesterday and said it was full. Frankie was already watering CJ when we broke through the trees.

"Not too much at one time, Frankie. You don't want CJ to get colic," Tommy said.

"I know," Frankie replied.

When John stepped off his horse, she let out this big sigh of relief. "She had been trying to do that all morning," John said. We all laughed and started watering the horses and got ready to eat.

We pulled all our lunches out of our saddlebags and laid out a blanket. "Just like a girl to bring a blanket to sit on," Frankie said, trying to be smart.

"Grandma said that if you lay a white blanket down and put your food on it, you can see if any bugs are coming to take your food," I told Frankie. "But you don't have to use it if you don't want to."

We all sat on the blanket to eat our lunch. Mom made chicken sandwiches, which everyone said were really good. "I got knocked out the last time I had one of these. Maybe this time I'll remember it,"

I said. We all started talking—about everything but me leaving. I knew it would be soon. But I didn't want to think about it.

"Hey, everyone. Come look at this. It wasn't here a minute ago." Mike called everyone over to the back of the creek. There was a red cooler. It definitely wasn't there earlier because we all had stood by the creek to look out at the water right before we decided to eat. "Mike, you open it. You found it," Tommy said while walking backward.

"No way, man. It could be something dead. I hate dead things. They stink—especially when it's been in there awhile." Mike was walking away.

"What if it's somebody's head!" Frankie said.

"What in the world, Frankie. You watch way too much television," John said, not looking like he wanted to open it either.

I went down, picked up the cooler, headed back up the bank, and set it down. With great caution, I opened it up. One thing was for sure: there was nothing dead in this cooler. I looked inside and couldn't take my eyes off of it. It was incredible. Tears rolled down my face.

Frankie came running up and said, "I told you it was somebody's head."

"Where does he get that crap?" said John, still amazed Frankie would say such things. Everyone looked into the cooler. I was trying to control my emotions.

A birthday cake—it was my first birthday cake, the only one I've ever had. It even had my name on it. It was beautiful. It was unbelievable. But where did it come from?

Frankie yelled out, "Wow, we got cake! Boy, am I glad it's not somebody's head."

"Frankie, stop it with the head, please," Tommy said. I didn't hear anything. It was so pretty; I didn't want this moment to end. "Did you guys know about this?" I asked.

"No, we didn't. This looks like something Grandma would do. She's pretty amazing," Tommy said.

Frankie jumped up and began, "I thought it was a—"

But Mike grabbed him and sat him down. "Enough, Frankie."

Frankie just grinned and said, "Let's eat cake."

Boy, I didn't want this day to end. It couldn't have been better.

But eventually, we had to pack everything up and get ready to go back. We had to return before dark, and it got dark early this time of year.

"Tommy, Tommy!" Frankie was running up from the creek. "Come look! Everyone come look!" Frankie was pointing down to the creek.

"What is it, Frankie?" Mike said.

Tommy and John walked over to the bank to see the birds flying in.

"Come on, everybody! Let's watch. I think the dolphins are coming in to feed." Tommy was all excited. He loved it when they fed on the bank. And I just thought the day couldn't get better.

All kinds of birds were starting to line the banks as we sat down next to them. We had a front-row seat. The birds didn't seem to mind. It was maybe ten minutes till we saw a school of fish heading our way. Then, all of a sudden, dolphins swam up onto the banks, catching the fish.

Fish everywhere. Birds catching fish. There must have been thirty dolphins. I'd never seen that many at one time. There were some dolphins, out a little, slapping their tails in the water to scare the fish toward the shore. They were taking turns coming on shore to eat the fish. They were talking to each other. It was crazy. It was fascinating. It was totally unbelievable. And I was sitting there watching it with four of the best friends I'd ever had. Happy Birthday to me, I thought.

***

On the way back, we rode side by side, Frankie in the middle. John's filly walked along like she was finally calmed down or just tired. Either way, it was nice just walking through those big oak trees.

We got back to the barn right as it was getting dark. Dad was waiting in the barn. "It's about time you all got back here," he said.

"But, Dad, you wouldn't believe what all happened," Tommy started. But then the smell of food took over.

Frankie jumped up. "I smell gumbo! Oh yeah. I know what gumbo smells like."

"Put these horses up, and meet me at the house. I already put feed and water in their stalls," Dad said as he headed for the house.

As we got closer to the house, I could see a car that I didn't recognize. A sick feeling came over my body. "Whose car is that?" I asked Tommy.

"I don't know," he said back.

As we got close, I could see that there were some people who I didn't think I knew. Mom and Dad had a fire in the firepit. It was a good night for a fire. A Black man stood up, and Jim was beside him.

Frankie ran over first. "Uncle Gary! You're here. Boy, have we missed you. How long are you going to be here? You don't look so good. What happened to you?" Frankie grabbed Gary around the neck. Gary gasped in pain.

Dad grabbed Frankie. "Hold on there, little man. Gary has been in an accident and is still hurt."

"I'm sorry," Frankie said.

I walked up slowly to the Black man, but when I saw it was Jessie, I also ran up, wrapping my arms around him. "Jessie how are you? I've missed you so much. Where's Mae?"

Mae stood up. "Scout, I'm here." I ran over to Mae to give her a big hug.

"You both look great," I told them. "Mae, when is the baby due?" I was looking at Mae. She was glowing.

"What are you talking about, Scout? I'm not pregnant." Mae looked shocked.

"I'm sorry, Mae. But you *are* pregnant. I know. You look like a mare in foal, all glowing and beautiful." And she was.

Mae blushed and said, "Stop it, Scout! I'm not pregnant."

"Oh yes you are, so you better get ready," Grandma chimed in.

"OK, Scout. What's it going to be, boy or girl?" Jessie jumped in. "Bring on the baby. I'm ready for it." Jessie was over the moon.

"Wait a minute, Jessie. I don't think I'm pregnant," Mae kept on saying.

"Oh yes you are, my pretty lady," Grandma said.

Mae, deep down, was starting to get excited also. What if I *am* pregnant? Oh my! she thought. "It's going to be a boy," I said. "And can we name him Willy? Willy needs a second chance at life." I was smiling. That was the first time in a long time I could smile and think of Willy. I walked over to Gary and said, "You look like crap, Gary. What happened to you?"

"Long story. But at least I look better than I did; I looked like death a few weeks ago. I'll take looking like crap over death," Gary said. I could tell he was really tired.

"Let's eat," Frankie came running over with a bowl of gumbo. "Best in the world." Frankie was chowing down.

"We have to give Scout her presents first, Frankie. Remember, it's her birthday," Mom said. Then she continued, "Jessie and Mae, these are our sons, since Scout didn't introduced them. This here is Tommy, John, Mike, and Frankie. Now, let's open presents and eat—maybe not in that order for Frankie, but that's OK." Frankie was eating like he had never eaten before.

I opened my presents. Mom and Dad gave me a book on Edisto, and Grandma gave me a book on natural medicines. Jessie and Mae brought me clothes. Then we got to eat.

Jessie got a bowl of Grandma's gumbo and said, "I know now why that little man couldn't wait. This is pure heaven. I've never had anything like this before." Mom and Grandma outdid themselves. We had crab cakes, steamed shrimp, cornbread, shrimp salad, regular salad, and green beans. We all ate till we couldn't eat anymore. Good thing—because there wasn't much left.

The boys and I were left with clean-up duty. Well, all but Frankie; he was sound asleep in a chair. We were taking things into the kitchen when Tommy asked me, "Why do you think that Jessie and Mae are here? Do you think they just brought Gary home?"

"Gary lives here? You never told me Gary lived here? I think that Jessie and Mae are here to take me back. I haven't asked them yet, but I'm sure. I guess I really didn't want to know. But Gary lives here?" I was amazed that no one ever mentioned it. "Where does he live—at Grandma's or here?" I didn't want to think about going back, so anything but that.

"He has a cabin in the woods, closer to the beach. And you never asked about him. He'll be staying at Grandma's till he gets better." Tommy was throwing things away and talking at the same time.

"I don't want to go back Tommy." Tears were forming in my eyes.

Tommy, Mike, and John walked over and gave me a hug and said, "We don't want you to go either." We finished cleaning up without saying another word.

* * *

Later that night when everyone had settled in, Mom pulled out the couch for Jessie and Mae to sleep on, and everyone else went to their rooms. Frankie had to be carried; he never woke up after eating. Everyone was tired.

I walked outside to sit on the swing and cry. Mom and Dad walked out and just sat with me for a while, then went inside. There wasn't much to say. Jessie came out later, must have been close to one in the morning, and sat down on the swing beside me. He looked at me and Jim and said, "Mae and I have really missed you, Scout. But we can see why you love it here. Maybe one day you'll get to come back. Gary was right when he sent you here. He said this was a special place. I didn't know he lived here also till we were driving here. We're going to have to leave early in the morning, so you better get some rest."

I didn't say a word—not out of disrespect...I didn't know what to say. Jessie got up and walked back into the house.

Jim and I sat there till the sun came up. I didn't want to miss a single minute that I had left here. This must be what death is like: when you leave everything you love.

Chapter 14

GOING BACK

It was still early when Frankie came outside and sat down beside me.

"What are you doing, Scout?" Frankie asked.

"Getting ready to leave," I answered.

"Where're you going?" Frankie asked.

"I have to go back with Jessie and Mae." I was holding back tears.

"Mom said you wouldn't have to go back till after Thanksgiving, remember?" Frankie's lip was starting to quiver.

"Things changed, my little friend. I have to go back today." Tears were now flowing down my face.

Frankie ran into the house. "Mom, tell Scout she can stay here. Tell her she can't go." Frankie couldn't stop crying. Neither could I at this point. Jessie and Mae walked into the kitchen, and Frankie unloaded on them. "I hate you! I hate you both because you're taking Scout away. I wish you had never come here!"

"Frankie!" Mom said. But Frankie ran out of the room before she could say anymore.

"We all are going to really miss her. Why does she have to go back anyway? Gary said that her parents could care less about her. So why does she have to go?" Mom was fighting back tears.

Grandma came walking through the back door into the kitchen. "Well, is there a reason for all this heartache?" Grandma chimed in.

Jessie felt trapped. "All I know is," he started, "when her parents were out of town, Scout came and lived in that old broodmare barn. She was all beat up by her brothers, she told me. So Mae and I fed and took care of her. Well, then all that mess happened, where that little Willy boy had gotten killed. Scout needed a safe place to go."

"Willy was killed in front of Scout? She never told us what had happened." Mom looked shocked.

"Yes, ma'am. Well, anyway, her parents were out of town, and so we sent her here. The case is pretty much closed on who killed Willy. And Lieutenant Glen and Gary just barely made it out alive. But anyhow, Scout's parents are back in town. Her brothers had gotten into some trouble with the neighbors, and the neighbors called the police, who in turn called social services. So, in reality, they just want Scout back to satisfy social services. Mae and I will always be there if she needs us. I promise that."

Jessie was being as honest as he could. Mae was standing next to him now, and all the boys were in the kitchen listening to him. I walked in and said, "We better get going. It's not going to get any easier." I walked into my room, gathered up my few things, and put them in my bag. Frankie was lying on my bed, crying his eyes out. "Frankie, I need you to do me a favor. Will you promise to do me this favor?" My tears were all dried up at the moment.

"No. You're leaving, and you aren't supposed to leave. This is your home." Frankie put his face into the pillow.

"Please, Frankie. I need your help. Please."

"OK what is it?" Frankie looked at me with a soaked face.

"Will you keep Jim for me till I get back? I'm coming back, Frankie. I promise." I didn't know when, but I was coming back.

"You promise you're coming back?" Frankie said.

"Yes. How could I leave my dog and my best friends and not come back? So will you take care of Jim for me, please?"

"OK. I will as long as you promise to come back."

"I will. Love you, Frankie." I grabbed my things, and Frankie and I walked out of my room.

Frankie walked up to Jessie. "I'm sorry, sir." And then he walked out the door.

Grandma walked over to give me a hug and said, "Girl, go in there and take a shower. You stink. They won't get ten miles before they stop and throw you in a creek. So get." It *had* been awhile since I had taken a shower. I hadn't even thought about it. I sniffed my shirt and wrinkled my nose. Boy, I did stink. Everyone laughed, and I left the room.

Grandma told Jessie, "Come, sit. Have a cup of coffee, and tell us the story of what happened. Scout hasn't said a word about it. Will she be OK when she gets back?"

Jessie and Mae sat down, and Jessie told the whole story. Even I just knew the beginning. Jessie would tell me the rest on the way home. Everyone but Frankie and I sat down to hear.

"OK," Grandma said, "what about this social services thing and Scout?"

"Scout has to go talk to the social worker next week. So she's going to stay with Sergeant Carson's family till then. After that, I don't know what happens to her, but I'll do whatever to make sure she's safe. I promise that." Jessie was sincere.

That shower was wonderful. It's amazing how much better you can feel when you're clean. I walked back into the kitchen, where everyone was still sitting at the table. "Do you want something to eat before you go?" Mom said to everyone.

Of course, the boys were starving, but I wasn't. I said no, and Jessie and Mae said it would probably be best to get on the road. Mom handed Jessie a cooler with food and drinks. "You might get hungry on the way."

"Scout, come here, please." Grandma was wanting another hug. "Girl, you sure do smell better."

"I feel a lot better too." And I did.

"Drink this for me, please, since you aren't going to eat. It is just some nutrition to keep you going." Grandma bent down and whispered in my ear, "I put some in their coffee."

As we walked out the door, Mom handed me a pillow and said, "We'll find a way to bring you home."

"I hope so," I replied.

Tommy, John, and Mike gave me a hug, and then things started getting real again. I was leaving. Tears rolled down my face. We got to the car, and here came Frankie and Jim. They both jumped in my arms and knocked me to the ground.

Frankie screamed, "You can't go! Please don't go! I want you to stay here! Please!" He was crying so hard.

I said, "I'll be back. I promise. You have to take care of Jim for me. Remember?" We were both crying.

Dad grabbed Frankie, and Tommy grabbed Jim. I got in the back seat, and Jessie and Mae got in the front. As we drove away, I looked back. Frankie chased the car until John got hold of him again. I looked at Jessie and Mae, and they had tears flowing down their faces.

"You know we love you don't you, Scout? You know we aren't taking you away from them because we want to? You know that, right?" Mae said, with tears rolling down her face.

"Oh yes, Mae. And I love the both of you. I was happy to see you. And thank you for the clothes." I had put them on after I took my shower. "I'm sorry. I guess I'm acting like a baby. It's just hard going back to what I know and leaving what I love…if that makes any sense. Nothing makes sense right now, but it's not your fault. I love you." We rode in silence for a while. The next thing I knew, I was waking up. I was tired. It had been a long twenty-four hours. We had pulled over to get something to eat.

"What do you want to eat, Scout?" Jessie said. It reminded me of my trip to Edisto with Tommy, when we stopped to get something to eat and all I could think about was the sandwich Mae had made for me—and how good that sandwich tasted because Mae made it for me. Now all I could think about was what Mom had made for me. All I wanted was whatever she had fixed.

"Jessie, can we stop at a rest area to eat what is in the cooler. I bet it will be good. Mom is like Mae. You won't go hungry."

So that's what we did. We ate and finally had time to talk. I told them about Mae's sandwich on the way here and now how I felt about Mom's food—which, by the way, was chicken sandwiches, slaw, fruit, chips, and drinks. But I had to tell them the story of the chicken sandwich and school. It was nice. I really did miss Jessie and Mae. I didn't realize how much till we sat down to eat and talk. They did tell me that I would be staying at the Carson's for a little while and that I had an appointment to see a social worker next week. I was glad to hear I wasn't going straight back to my parents.

When we got back into the car, Mae got in the back seat so she could rest. Jessie asked, "Why did you leave Jim behind, Scout?"

"Well, if I end up back at the house with my parents, they won't let me have a dog or any pet. Frankie will take good care of him, and Jim likes it there. So did I." I felt sad. "What happened after I left, Jessie?"

Jessie proceeded to tell me the whole story, which, by the way, took a long time. We were stopping for gas again when he finished, and Mae was waking up. "Did anyone ever figure out who Willy was and where he came from?" I asked.

Jessie said, "No," with a sad look on his face.

"Was there a funeral for him?" I asked.

Jessie just shook his head. "No."

"That just don't seem right, Jessie. No one said goodbye to him. Do you know where he is?"

"You can ask Bobby all those questions when you see him." Jessie didn't want to think about him anymore.

After getting gas, we loaded back into the car and headed down the road, and for the rest of the ride, we let the past be the past. We listened to the radio and sang to the songs we knew. And too soon we were back to where it all started.

Chapter 15

BOBBY'S HOUSE

When we got to the Carson house, it was getting dark. We drove up, and I could see Bobby's truck in the driveway. We got out and walked to the house. Jessie knocked on the door. When the door opened, it was Carol, her face just gleaming.

"Come in," she said as she ran into the kitchen. We followed.

"You want some chicken, anyone?" Bobby looked up from his bucket of fried chicken. "I have enough for everyone."

Mae looked around at the mess: dirty dishes, dirty clothes, newspapers. "Where is Sue?" Mae asked.

"Mom has been sick for a while now. So Dad has been taking care of us," Carol said.

"Bobby?" Mae looked at him.

"We don't know what's going on. We've been to the doctors twice now, but they don't know why she's sick. She has another doctor's appointment next week. But, no worries. Carol and I are going to get this place cleaned up. Isn't that right, Carol?" Bobby said. You could tell he was worried and worn out.

"Well, I'll tell you what: Scout here and I are going to clean the house tomorrow for you. You should have told me you needed help," Mae said, looking at Bobby.

"Mae, to tell you the truth, I don't know how it got this way. One day it's clean, and then all of a sudden you get this. I don't when or how this happened?" Bobby threw his hands in the air. Everyone laughed.

"We're going if that's OK, Bobby. I'm so tired. I can hardly keep my eyes open," Jessie said and started toward the door.

"I'll be back in the morning," Mae said, following Jessie.

"Jessie, wait." Bobby walked over and handed him a folder with some papers in it. "Take a look at this when you get a chance, and let me know," he said as he walked away.

"What's this, Bobby?" Jessie asked.

"When you get a chance, look at it. It's only important if you're interested." Bobby walked back into the kitchen.

Jessie was too tired to care, so he just took the folder, and he and Mae walked out the door.

"Hi, Scout. How've you been?" Bobby said, realizing he hadn't even said hello to her yet.

"OK." I was pretty tired myself.

"Dad, Mom wants you." Carol stood in the kitchen door.

"OK." He was walking out of the kitchen and looked back. "You all eat some chicken, please."

Carol and I looked at each other and said, "Yes, sir," at the same time.

＊＊＊

That night, I couldn't sleep. I kept thinking about everyone on the island, and I really missed Jim. I knew he was better off there, but, boy, did I miss him. To keep from tossing and turning, I got up and went into the kitchen and started cleaning up. It was a mess. I cleaned till I heard Bobby get up and go in Carol's room to wake her for school. I got back on the couch and acted like I was asleep. I didn't feel like talking. Bobby walked into the kitchen and couldn't believe his eyes. He came to the den to thank me, but I didn't move. He didn't want to bother me, so he sat down and wrote me and Mae a note and put it on the table with his credit card. Carol walked into the kitchen and said, "This isn't our house! It doesn't even smell like fried chicken anymore. Thank goodness."

"We're running late, Carol. Let's get in the car, and I'll get you something to eat along the way," Bobby said while holding the door open for her.

"I hope you don't stop for fried chicken," Carol said, with a smirk.

"Get in the car," Bobby said, as he put his arm around Carol. And off they went.

I must have fallen asleep because the next thing I remember was a knock on the door. I got up to see, and it was Mae. "Girl, you must have been sound asleep, because I've been knocking for about five minutes. Didn't want to ring the doorbell and bother Sue."My mind was still a fog. "Sorry, Mae" was all I could think to say.

"Have you checked on Sue? How sick is she?" Mae said with concern.

"I haven't gone in there. Should I?"

"I don't know."

I hadn't even thought about it.

We both walked back to the master bedroom and opened the door. Sue was in a fetal position. She looked up.

Mae said, "Sue, if you need anything, you let us know. And we'll be checking on you. Do you want anything while we're here? Sue, you look awful." Mae walked over to the bed. "Scout, go get some ice water, please." I got the water from the kitchen and handed it to Mae. "We'll be here if you need us, and I'll check on you in a little while." Mae and I walked out of the room.

We went into the kitchen, and Mae couldn't believe her eyes. "Who did this?" Mae asked.

"Couldn't sleep. Had to do something. The rest is still a big mess," I reassured her. I looked on the table and saw the note Bobby left and his credit card. The note said, *If you could do me a big favor and go to the grocery store and get some things. We are out of everything—toilet paper, paper towels, milk, food—everything. You may want to first list things. I don't think I have much as far as cleaning supplies. Have a great day! And thank you! The keys to Sue's car are hanging on the wall by the door.*

"OK then, Scout. Let's make us a grocery list. You check the refrigerator, and I'll check the bathrooms and for cleaning supplies." Mae was getting cranked up. I opened the refrigerator, and all I saw was fried chicken.

"Can I throw all this crap away?" I asked Mae in disgust.

"Sure thing. And check the labels on everything in there. No telling how long it's been there."

I ended up cleaning everything out of the refrigerator, a lot of trash. "Can we go to the dump and throw all this trash away?" I asked Mae.

"Bag it good, girl, because I don't want it to leak in that car. But yes, we need to get rid of it, or it will stink to high heaven if we put it outside."

We got our list together and headed to the dump to throw out all this stuff. We got the trash thrown out and headed to the store.

"What was in the folder Bobby gave Jessie last night, Mae?" I asked.

"I don't know. He hasn't looked at it yet. Jessie's been working part-time for a timber company. He likes it too; they pay decent. We're looking for a house to rent. There's a lot going on right now. It's strange how one day everything seems hunky-dory and the next the whole world changes." Mae stared at the road, like she was somewhere else.

"You OK, Mae?" I asked.

"Yes. I'm fine, Scout," Mae said with a smile.

"Do you think Bobby would mind if I got some extra things to make Sue a soup? Miss Winnie at Edisto showed me how to make a healing soup." I couldn't make myself call her Grandma since wasn't there and didn't know if I would ever be there again.

"I don't think he'd mind," Mae answered.

At the store we decided to split up. I went to get the things I needed for my soup with a list Mae gave me for meats and vegetables. Mae went to get cleaning supplies and paper items (toilet paper, paper towels). Mae also got paper plates; maybe they can find the trash can, since the dishes didn't ever get washed. It wasn't long before we were at the register with two big buggies of stuff. We looked at each other and said, "Oh well." We loaded everything in the car and headed back to the house.

After unloading and putting everything up, we checked on Sue and started cleaning. After a while we were starving. We made us some sandwiches and tea. Mae started some beef stew for Bobby and asked me, "Can you make rice, Scout?"

"Yes, and I also got some vegetables I can make," I said.

"Well, Jessie will be here soon to pick me up, and I'll be back tomorrow to help you finish up." Mae looked tired.

"You need to go see a doctor, Mae, and check on that baby." I was a little concerned.

There was a knock on the door. It was Jessie. We let him in, and he gave me a hug and looked at Mae and said, "We need to go, Mae."

"What's the hurry, Jessie?" I asked.

"Unless you young ladies made enough of that good-smelling food for everyone, we got to go. I'm starving."

Mae ran over to the counter and made Jessie a sandwich. "This should hold you till we get home." She handed Jessie the sandwich and a paper cup of tea. "See you tomorrow, Scout," Mae said as they headed out the door.

I started getting things together to make Sue some soup. The store had most of what I needed. It would have to do. Mae's stew was smelling really good; it was hard to concentrate. I got my soup going and started planning the rest of the meal. I started the rice and was looking at the vegetables that I got, not sure what anyone liked.

After the rice was done, I went back to check on Sue. She looked so weak lying in the bed. But she was awake. "Can I get you anything, Sue," I asked.

"Hi, Scout. I heard you were coming. So when did you get here?" Sue said in a weak voice.

"Last night," I answered.

"Good to see you, Scout. Is Mae still here?" "No, she left awhile ago. Can I do something for you?"

"Oh yes. Could I get some ice water, please?" She was so weak.

"Yes. I'll be right back." I took her glass by the bed, which had water in it—she hadn't drunk much—and went into the kitchen. I took a glass full of ice and a little water, as well as a cup of my soup, back to the room. I walked back into the bedroom with everything on a tray, with soup crackers and the water.

"What's all this?" Sue asked.

I figured she wouldn't eat it if I told her I'd made it, so I said, "Mae made you some soup. She thought it might make you feel better. She said you need to eat something."

"Well, since Mae went through the trouble, I'll try it. I haven't wanted to eat anything for a while, but this smells delightful," Sue said. That made me happy. Sue ate most of the soup, laid her head on the pillow, and went back to sleep. This time, she looked comfortable and not all knotted up. Before I left the room, Sue was fast asleep.

While she slept, I cleaned the master bathroom, the last place we had to clean. Then, I went into the kitchen to fix some rice for dinner. I didn't know what kind of vegetable they would like, so I took some broccoli and made a salad. Close to six o'clock, Bobby and Carol walked in. I figured Carol would have ridden the bus home. Then Bobby spoke up, not happy at all. "Carol, here, missed her bus, and her friend who lives all the way across town took her home with her and called me when they got there. I still think this was planned. You just wanted to spend time with your friend."

Carol, with a grin, looked at Scout. As she walked toward her room, she said, "Oh, Dad. I can't believe you would think that." She closed the door but then opened it up right away. "Is that food? Like, real food, not fried chicken? Dad, I smell food, real food. Dad, we've gone to the wrong house."

Bobby stopped a minute. "Oh my...Oh my! I smell it too." And they both drifted into the kitchen and sat down at the table. I was in the kitchen putting everything on the table when they walked in. All I said was "Let's eat," and the talking stopped.

After a little while, Carol looked at her dad and said, "Sorry, Dad. It was planned, and I'll never do it again. It has just been tough around here with Mom sick and all. I'm really sorry."

Bobby looked up from his plate at Carol. With a mouthful of food, he mumbled, "Thank you. We got this, Carol. Everything's going to be OK. I love you, Carol." Then he looked at me. "Who made this? Oh my god, this is good. I only wish Sue could eat something. How is she doing today?" He stopped eating and got up to go check on her.

I said, "Sue did eat some soup today. She said she liked it."

"Really, Scout? That's great news." Bobby headed down the hall and yelled back, "Don't touch anything; I'm not done eating." He walked into the bedroom, then back into the kitchen. With a smile he said, "Sue said she wanted some more soup. This is wonderful. She hasn't eaten a bite in days. When she would try, it wouldn't stay down. She said Mae made a special soup for her."

I handed him a bowl of my soup and sent him on his way. He came back to the kitchen later with an empty bowl in his hand and said, "She ate every bit of this soup. I watched her take every bite. It was wonderful. And now she's fallen asleep. She ate every bit of it." He was very pleased. He fixed himself another plate and started eating again. Now that Sue had eaten something, he didn't feel so guilty.

Bobby got up from the table and looked around. "Scout," he said, "you and Mae did a fine job. The house looks great. Thank you."

"Thanks," I said. "But we still have a lot of washing to do. We'll get that done tomorrow." The house did look a lot better and smelled a heap better too.

Carol got up from the table and said, "I'm going to take a bath, do homework, and go to bed. Goodnight, Dad. Goodnight, Scout. Thanks for real food. It was good." Carol walked into her room, grabbed her nightclothes, and went into the bathroom.

I started cleaning up the kitchen. Bobby was helping. "You OK, Scout? I haven't had much time to talk to you. How was that island you were on? You feel like talking?" "Not really—I'm really tired. Can we talk another day? I was going to clean this up, take a shower myself, and go to bed. Is that OK?" I didn't want to hurt his feelings.

"That's OK, Scout. I'm tired also; it's been a long day. But it's good to see you again, and we'll talk later." He put down a dish towel. The dishes were done, and we both walked off in silence.

I went into the guest room, where I was staying, and looked around at all the stuff. The bed was cleaned off, and a path from the door to the bed was cleared. I looked around for something to sleep in. I didn't have many clothes but didn't want to sleep in my only clean clothes. I looked in one of the many boxes and found a big t-shirt. "Perfect," I said to myself. I went and took my shower and then crawled into bed.

Chapter 16

SUE

When I woke up the next morning, everything was quiet, so I thought it was early. I walked into the kitchen and realized that Bobby and Carol were already gone. I looked on the table, and there was a note. This must be the way they communicate around here. The note read, *Here is my phone number: 990-2222. Call me if you or Sue needs anything. I may be home for lunch to eat leftovers. Jessie called and said Mae wasn't feeling well, and they're going to the doctor.*

"Well, you know what that means," I said to myself. "Baby time."

I put a load of clothes into the washer and started to make Sue something to eat. I cooked some grits, put the rest of the soup in it, and scrambled two eggs. I also made toast and poured some orange juice.

I walked into Sue's bedroom and saw she was asleep. But she still needs to eat, so I went over to the bed. "Sue, wake up. I got some breakfast for you, and you have to take your medicines." I saw the meds on the side table, and it said when it was to be taken.

Sue looked up, still very weak but not as pale. "Thank you, Scout. I think I'll try to eat a little. Is Mae here? Did she make breakfast? Have you eaten?" Boy, those were a lot of questions for a sick lady.

I wasn't sure what to say. "Mae stopped by and made breakfast, but she had a doctor's appointment and had to go. But she said I needed to remind you to take your medicines and eat." I didn't know why, but I didn't think she would eat if she knew I fixed it. Anyway, what difference does it make as long as she eats?

I helped sit Sue up in bed and put the tray in front of her. "This looks wonderful, Scout. Thank you." I watched Sue take her first bite. She looked pleased, so I left to go do more laundry.

Later I checked on Sue again, and she was fast asleep. So I took the tray back to the kitchen, pleased to see she had eaten most of it. Then I went into Carol's room, stripped the bed, and put clean sheets on. Then I got her towel and all the dirty clothes that were on the floor and headed back to do laundry. It just kept piling up.

After a while I went back into Sue's room, and she was still asleep. I walked into her bathroom and picked up some (I had cleaned it yesterday), and I started running water into the bathtub. She needed a bath; the smell in the room was of sickness. If I could get her into the tub, change the bedsheets, and get Sue into some clean night-clothes, I thought she would feel a little better—at least smell better. Plus she had a doctor's appointment tomorrow. She needed a bath.

I walked back to the bed to wake Sue, pleased with my decision. But first I wanted to put some herbs in the tub to draw out poison from the body. I read about it in the book Grandma gave me for my birthday. I woke Sue up. "Come on, Sue. You need to take a bath. You have a doctor's appointment tomorrow, and you want to be clean—and Mae said so." I was hoping that would encourage her a little more.

Sue got out of bed, and I helped her to the bathroom. As soon as she walked through the door, she said, "What's that wonderful smell?"

"Come on, Sue. Let's get this gown off and get you into the tub. You'll feel so much better after this bath."

Sue did as she was told, and when she stepped into the tub, you would have thought it was the first bath she ever had. She sat down and lay back, with her head on the edge of the tub. I asked her to sit up so I could wash her hair. It was bad. I had never washed anybody's hair. But how hard could it be? When I finished, Sue lay back again.

"Here's a washrag and some soap. Wash the rest of yourself, and I'll be back soon. Don't fall asleep in the tub, please." I was scared to leave her.

Sue picked her hand up and waved me away. "I got this, Scout. You can go."

I went back into the bedroom, changed the sheets, and found a clean bedspread to go on top. I went around and wiped up everything and vacuumed the floors. Then I went back into the bathroom, where Sue was just about to fall asleep. "Come on, Sue. Let's get up and dried off. Bobby said he may be here for lunch, and it's almost lunchtime."

Sue said, "OK," and slowly stood up out of the tub. I wrapped her in a towel and had her sit down so I could dry her hair. It wasn't long before her hair was dry and she was in a clean nightgown. I got her back into the bed.

"I don't think I've ever had a bath that felt that good. Is there any soup left? I would love some more." She was looking much better.

"I'll go see. Get some rest, and I'll bring you some soup in a little while." Sue lay back in her clean bed, closed her eyes, and said, "OK," as she drifted to sleep.

I went into the kitchen and started warming leftovers and making soup. This was a different soup, but I thought she would like it. It was almost one o'clock. I thought maybe Bobby wasn't going to be here for lunch, and I got Sue's tray ready. As I was fixing to take Sue her tray, Bobby walked into the house.

"What you got there, Scout?" he asked.

"Taking Sue some lunch. I warmed up those leftovers, if you want some." I headed to the bedroom.

Sue was awake when I went in, already sitting up in bed and waiting for lunch. As I was getting her tray situated on the bed, Bobby walked in with his own tray, looked at Sue, and asked, "Mind if I join you?" He couldn't believe how much better she looked.

"But of course," Sue replied, with a smile on her face.

Bobby sat down on the bed next to Sue, and they both started eating, while just looking at each other.

Well, this is awkward, I thought. So I left the room. I don't think anybody noticed.

I went into the kitchen and fixed myself something to eat. Mae was a good cook; the leftover stew was so good. One thing I could say for sure: I had some good food lately. If I had to go back to live with my parents and brother, I would starve. No one in that house cooked; it was all fast food. I hoped I didn't have to go back there.

I was daydreaming while eating my stew, when Bobby walked back into the kitchen, carrying both trays. He said, "Scout, I don't know what you're doing, but keep it up. That's the best Sue has looked in weeks. Look, Scout. We have to have a talk tonight when I get home. There's a lot we need to discuss. You're going to be OK. I promise. Your best interests are all we care about." He looked around. "Have you heard from Mae today, Scout?"

"No. Why do you ask? You left a note and said she had to go to the doctor." I was feeling like I might have done something wrong.

"Sue said Mae was here this morning and made her breakfast and more soup. So was Mae here today?" Bobby was a policeman. What could I say? I knew what was going on.

"No. I just told Sue that because I was scared she wouldn't eat if she thought I made it. Winnie, back on the island, showed me how to make all kinds of soups—for healing...and just good soup. I started making it for Sue yesterday, after Mae left."

I could see Bobby wasn't angry, just curious. "Well, it has made a big difference on Sue. Thank you so much—and that Winnie lady too." With that, he headed to the door. He stopped, looked back, and said, "You want me to stop and get some friend chicken on the way home this evening?"

"Please, please, no buckets of chicken! I got this. No worries," I said with a grin. I did like Bobby. He was a nice man. At first I didn't like him at all. But he did grow on me, and he was a good father and husband.

That night I did make chicken and dumplings for dinner. Bobby and Carol came walking through the door before five.

"Got off early today?" I asked.

"No. When Carol doesn't run off, we get here about this time in the evenings. Usually her mom takes care of her, but since she's been sick, I have to do it"—he looked at Carol with love—"and I don't mind a bit."

"Boy, something smells good!" Carol said, with bright eyes looking for the food.

"It's not ready yet, but all the clothes are washed and put up. Supper will be ready soon," I said, all proud of myself.

Carol went to her room to put up her books. She looked around the room and in her closet and in her dresser drawer. Then she returned to the kitchen and gave me a big hug.

"What's that for?" I asked. Bobby was wondering also.

"My room—it's all clean. I have clean clothes, and my bed is all clean, just like Mom does it. Thank you! Yay! I have clean clothes again." And she headed back toward her room.

"You've always had clean clothes, and you're old enough to clean your own room," Bobby called after her.

But she didn't listen. She just went into her room and yelled back, "Let me know when it's time to eat. I'm starving!" With that, she closed the door.

"You've done a remarkable job, Scout. Thank you," Bobby said to me.Just then, the phone rang. I had been here almost two days, and this was the first time I heard the house phone ring. Everyone has cell phones, I'd guessed.

Bobby answered the phone. "Hello? Yes how are you?...What did the doctor say?...Really? That's great news!...Scout has everything cleaned up and looking good. I have to take Sue back to the doctor's tomorrow, so maybe you can come by, and you and Scout could go look at baby clothes. You can take Sue's car, and I know Scout would love to get out of this house a little. Would you mind?...Sounds great." He hung up the phone. "That was Mae. She *is* pregnant. I'm so glad for them. Anyway, she's coming to take you out of the house for a while tomorrow while I take Sue to the doctor. Does that sound OK to you, Scout?"

"Yes. It would be good to get out a little. I *told* her she was going to have a baby. That's exciting!" I was happy for her.

It was time to eat. I set the table and fixed Sue something to eat and put it on a tray.

Bobby said, "Fix me a tray also; I'll eat in the bedroom with Sue." But as soon as I got the table set, here came Sue, walking into the kitchen.

"You got room for one more?" Sue said.

Bobby was glowing. "Look at you, Sue! You look beautiful!"

"I know I look like hell, but I do feel better." Sue said with a smile. "What smells so good in here?" She was hungry. Carol walked into the kitchen to eat and saw her mom. She ran over and gave her a hug. Carol was so excited to see her up and about that she started crying. "Why are you crying, Carol? I'm OK." Sue was trying to calm her down.

"You were in the bed so long I didn't know if you would ever get better." Carol was really sobbing now. "Come, come now. It's OK. Now stop all this crying, and let's eat. We'll all eat together. It's been a long time since we've all eaten together." Everyone sat down at the table and ate and talked. And Bobby looked plum relieved. We ate all the chicken and dumplings, cornbread, and salad. It was good, even if I say so myself.

After dinner Sue went back to bed. Bobby told Carol to go do her homework and look after her mom and that we would be back soon.

"Where are you going?" said Carol.

"Scout and I have to go see Lieutenant Glen," Bobby answered.

"Is he still in the hospital?" Carol asked.

"No. He's staying with his sister till he gets better." "OK. Tell him I hope he gets better soon." She went to her room and shut the door.

While in the car driving to go see Lieutenant Glen, Bobby asked, "You've not said much about that place where you were. And I thought you'd be asking all kinds of questions about what happened after you left and that dog of yours. I didn't think you'd go anywhere without him." Bobby found himself full of questions.

"The place where I was at was nice. The people there were real nice too. Jessie told me all of what had happened here, and it was awful. It made me real sad that the Hunters hurt all those people and horses. I don't really know what to say about it. But what I do know is if I have to go back to my parents, they won't let me have a dog. And Jim is happy where he is." That was all I knew to say.

"What did you do at that place?" Bobby asked.

"Nothing much. It all seems like a dream now," I told him, "a really good dream.""Well, I'm glad you were safe."

Chapter 17

WHAT TO DO

We pulled into a driveway at a very nice house in a very nice neighborhood.

"This doesn't look like a place Lieutenant Glen would live," I said to Bobby.

"He doesn't live here. But since he got out of the hospital, he's staying here till he's better. This is his sister's house. Her husband is in the navy and is gone a lot. I know he's an officer, but I don't know what rank—must be pretty high up to afford this place. Wouldn't you say?" Bobby looked at the house.

"At least he has a nice place to stay while he's getting better," I said as we were getting out of the car.

We walked up to and onto the porch. It was a big house with one of those wraparound porches that goes all the way around the house. I could live on the porch, I thought. As Bobby reached to ring the doorbell, the door flew open. It startled both of us as well as the lady at the door.

"Oh! Hi, Bobby. Adam is in the den waiting for you. Just walk on in. Vic and I have to go to the store, so we'll be back soon. Be careful; I'm leaving Mary Beth here, and she can get to be a pain. Just don't shoot her before I get back." As she was walking away—with this tall, nice-looking young man at her arm—she looked back and said, "Go on in. He's in the den."

"Who was that?" I asked.

"That's Lieutenant Glen's sister and her oldest child. Evidently, she left the daughter here. The son calls her a 'sour pickle.' Don't rightly know what that means, but I guess we'll find out. Come on, Scout." Bobby walked into the house, but I was watching that lady and boy get into the car and drive away. "Come on, Scout," Bobby said again while holding the door open. Something about that boy...He just hung on my mind for some reason. Grandma told me that there were all kinds of people in this world, and she said that there were helpers like Willy and Tommy, and there were healers like Grandma, and there were searchers, and there were onlookers who could see things, things that are going to happen. I wondered what the tall boy was. "Last call. Come on, Scout!" Bobby wasn't happy.

"I'm sorry. I'm coming."

We went into the huge house.

"Do you know where we're going, Bobby? This place is big." I was looking at the entrance of the house.

A cute little girl walked up and said, "Who are you? And why are you in my house?" All the cuteness went away.

"You must be Mary Beth. I'm Bobby, and this is Scout. We're look-ing for your uncle. Can you show us where he is, please?" Bobby looked like he could smack her.

"Whatever. Come on. I'll show you." Mary Beth pranced her butt right down the hallway. She stopped at an open door and said, "Uncle Adam, someone here to see you. I think it's too late to have anyone over. It's almost my bedtime."

Lieutenant Glen looked at the little girl and said, "Please feel free to go to bed, and I promise we won't bother you." Lieutenant Glen looked at Bobby and me and said, "You all, come on in and sit down."

"What is this 'you all' stuff? You would think there was a whole lot of people." Mary Beth muttered as she went down the hallway and left.

"Scout, how are you? You OK? Everything go OK where you were? You look good. I'm just glad to see you," Lieutenant Glen said.

"I'm fine. All is good. But you don't look so good," I said to Lieutenant Glen. And he didn't look good at all.

"I *am* looking good. You should have seen me four weeks ago. That was when I looked really bad." Lieutenant Glen and Bobby both laughed.

"OK, Scout. I had Bobby bring you here so we could talk about what's best for you. We may need you to testify in court. Will you be OK with that?"

I said, "Yes, I could do that."

"You have to meet with a social worker this coming Monday. Do you think Mae could take her to that, Bobby?" Lieutenant Glen had a list of things he wanted done written on a piece of paper in front of him.

"If Mae can't, then I'll take her there," Bobby answered.

"Your parents want you back because social services were called on your brothers, and they wanted to know where you are. Your parents said that you ran away. I straightened that out, but social services want to talk to you. What do you want, Scout? Do you want to go back to your parents?" Lieutenant Glen looked tired.

"I'll do whatever I'm told. I don't want to cause any more trouble. I can go back to my parents because I have nowhere else to go. It will be OK." I knew they would beat the crap out of me for leaving in the first place. "You would tell me if they would hurt you in any way, right?" Lieutenant Glen said.

"Yes, I would." I had to lie. I'm not their responsibility. We stayed just a little longer and were heading out the door when Lieutenant Glen's sister came walking in. Her son was carrying in some bags of groceries. And with a quick "hello" and "goodbye," we left.

As we were driving back to Bobby's house, I asked him, "What do you know about that boy? Or man? He didn't look that old, just big."

"Not much. But he does some strange things. Lieutenant Glen said he was autistic—which, from my understanding, is a mental development." Bobby was getting flustered. "He can do real strange things. Like, he told me before Sue got sick that I needed to take her to the doctor. And the next thing you know, Sue is sick, and we are going to the doctor."

"Miss Winnie said they are called onlookers. They can see things that may happen," I told Bobby.

He looked at me and said, "I want to meet this Miss Winnie. She sounds like a pretty interesting person. "I said to myself, "I just want to go back."

***

The rest of the drive was quiet. We got back to Bobby's house and walked inside. Everyone had gone to bed. He patted me on the shoulder and said, "Good night, Scout," and headed to his room. He stopped, looked over his shoulder, and said, "Would you want to live here, Scout? Would you think about it?" He walked into the bedroom before I could answer. But I think that was the idea—he wanted me to think about it.

Boy, did I ever think about it. What did he mean? Was there a way I wouldn't have to go back to my parents? Was that fair to say I wanted to stay here, when I didn't know what I wanted? But that wasn't even a thought. But it was a good thought; I could like the thought. Mae would be here tomorrow, and I would talk to her and see what see thought.

Needless to say, it was a long night. I thought about everyone I knew. I missed everyone at Edisto. I wanted to go back so bad.

I finally fell asleep, and Willy was there. He told me I needed a break and said, "Come on. Let's go have fun."

Fun? How could I have fun with all this stuff on my mind? "But it is a dream, you know." That's what Grandma would say. So Willy and I rode horses, swam in the clearest of waters, and flew over land. It was a beautiful dream.

THE GIRL WHO NEVER WAS

Then the phone rang. So I woke up, walked into the kitchen, and answered it. "Hello?" I said with a sleepy voice.

"Scout, this is Grandma."

I could only say, "Grandma! Oh, I miss you so much. How is everyone and—"

"Stop, Scout. Hang in there. I've not given up. Your time will come. Love you. "Bobby walked into the kitchen. "Who's on the phone, Scout?"

"Grandma, I think." I was staring at the phone, and all I heard was a dial tone.

"I didn't even hear the phone ring," Bobby said, looking a little suspicious.

"Maybe I was dreaming? I don't know. Sorry." I did feel as though I'd been asleep. Now something else to have to think about—just what I needed.

"Who is your Grandma? I've never heard you talk about a Grandma." Bobby was looking at me strange.

"The boys who live at the place where I was called Miss Winnie Grandma, so I did too sometimes. I just think I was dreaming." I had nothing else to say, so I walked back into my room and got dressed.

It wasn't long before there was a knock on the door. I knew it was Mae. Bobby and family were fixing to leave. They were going to take Carol to school and then go to the doctor. They all met at the door.

"Sue, you look so much better," Mae said.

"It was that soup you made for me, Mae. That was the best soup I ever had," Sue said.

"I didn't make that soup; Scout did," Mae replied.

"Who?" Sue said.

Then Bobby said, "Come on, Sue. We're going to be late. Let's go." As the three headed for the car, Jessie handed Bobby the folder that Bobby gave him the other night. "Well, what do you think?" Bobby asked Jessie.

"I think it is worth a try, and I think I would like it," Jessie said.

"What's in the folder?" I asked Mae.

"An application to join the police department. I think Jessie would make a good policeman. Anyway, he is already signed up to start at the academy in December. Bobby already had him approved; Jessie just had to sign the paperwork." Mae was looking at Jessie so proud.

"That's wonderful Mae. I think Jessie would be a great policeman."

Everyone left except Mae and me. "Come on, Scout. Let's go check things out." Mae was excited. We got the keys and headed to town. "Why did Sue say I made the soup, Scout?" Mae asked. "I was afraid she wouldn't eat it if I told her I made it," I told Mae.

"She sure sounded strange to me, but she looked a whole lot better. I was glad to see that." Mae continued, "Did I tell you I think we found us a house to rent right now? We can maybe buy it later if this police thing works out."

"That sounds great! Can we go see it?" I asked.

"That's our first stop." Mae was happy.

We arrived at this cute little house on about two acres of land. It had two bedrooms and one bathroom. Then we went shopping and looking at baby things. After a while we had lunch at a hamburger place and went looking at things some more. Neither one of us had any money, but it was fun getting out of the house. By late afternoon we headed back to Bobby's house.

When we got back to the house, Bobby was there with Sue. We walked in, and no one was saying anything.

"Is everything all right?" Mae asked, thinking the worse. "Is there anything I can do for you?"Jessie came to the door. He walked in the house and asked, "What's going on?""I don't know," Mae said. "Scout and I walked in, and they were sitting on the couch not saying anything. I have asked a couple of times, and they just look at each other."

With that, Bobby and Sue broke out laughing. They laughed so hard tears were falling down their cheeks.

"What is it?" Mae asked again, not feeling as nervous as before.

"Sue is pregnant," Bobby said, glowing. "Whatever she had going on before is better. The doctor thinks everything will be OK."

Carol walked into the house from the bus stop and said, "What's going on here? How's Mom? Mom, you OK? What did the doctor say?" Carol was getting all worked up thinking she missed something.

"We are going to have a baby," Sue said, almost singing.

"Really!" Carol was beside herself.

"Yes, but I still need my rest. I'm worn out. I'm going to bed. See everyone later." Sue got up, still weak, and headed to the bedroom.

Chapter 18

JUDGMENT DAY

Over the rest of the quiet week, Sue got better every day. Everyone talked about Thanksgiving, which was the next week. I had an appointment with a social worker on Monday. Bobby hadn't mentioned a word about wanting me to stay. I think the baby had all their attention now. It was exciting–Mae and Sue having babies. But I sure did miss everyone on the island. I felt like I belonged there, not here. I loved Mae and Jessie, and I liked Bobby, Sue, and Carol. I appreciated all they had done for me, but I didn't belong here. I knew this; I felt it in my heart and soul.

The sun was coming up, and I was going to go for a walk. No one seemed to know that I was around anyway. I needed to stop feeling sorry for myself. Maybe a long walk would do me good. I got up, put on my clothes, grabbed my coat, and went on my way. I walked out the door, got about a block from the house, and realized it was freezing. I turned around, went back to the house, and told myself I didn't belong here.

As I was walking back inside the house, Bobby, Carol, and Sue were fixing to walk out the door. Carol and Sue walked by without saying a word to me, just talking to each other. Bobby stopped and said, "We're going to my mom and dad to tell them about the baby. We were going to wait till Thanksgiving but decided to go tell them today. Will you be all right by yourself?"

"Yes, I'll be fine," I told him.

Jessie and Mae came by and asked if I wanted to go eat lunch and then help them move.

"You got the house?" I asked.

"Yes, we did. I couldn't be happier," Mae said.

So I said, "OK, let's go move."

We first went to lunch, and then we started moving boxes. "I never unpacked the boxes for when we left the other house, so at least most of the things are still packed. Scout, you grab those boxes, and I'll get these." Mae was pointing at the different stacks of boxes.

"Oh no you don't." Jessie grabbed Mae by the arm. "You aren't going to hurt yourself carrying these heavy boxes. I got this. Scout and I can handle this. Just tell us which boxes you want to take first, and you can unpack them at the new place."

"I'm OK, Jessie," Mae replied.

"The doctor said no heavy lifting. Please let me and Scout do this." Jessie was insistent.

"OK, OK. I'll show you which boxes I want first," Mae complied to Jessie's wishes. We moved boxes all day.

By the time I got back to Bobby's house, I was exhausted.

No one was home yet, so I grabbed a glass of milk and headed to my room. I really didn't want to be in the way when they got home. The next morning was Sunday, and by the time I got up, Bobby and his family had gone to church. It was almost as though I wasn't even there. It was starting to get creepy. Well, the next day would be Monday. I would talk to the social worker and go back to my parents. My parents knew where I was. You would have thought they would have called or come by. Not them. I didn't want to go back there, but I didn't know what else I could do.

It was getting to be around noon on Sunday. I fixed myself something to eat, then headed out the door, only to bump into Bobby and family walking in with a big bucket of chicken. Man, they must love that stuff.

"You want some chicken, Scout? We got plenty," Bobby said, with a big grin on his face. Carol and Sue just walked right by, without saying a word, and headed for the kitchen.

"No thanks. I already had something to eat. If it's OK, I'm going for a walk before it gets too cold. Is that OK?"

"Suit yourself, kiddo. Just be careful." Bobby was so happy about the baby. He headed into the house with his bucket of chicken and all the fixings. It was a wonder that they weren't bigger than they were. They were still overweight, but with all that chicken, they should've weighed a ton. Well, they liked it, and that was all that mattered. I was on my way.

The day turned into a beautiful one. The leaves had fallen off the trees, and the grass was all brown. Everything looked dead. It was kind of sad. But the sun was bright and warm. The wind wasn't blowing, so while it was around forty degrees, it was nice.

As I was walking, I noticed Willy by my side. "Thanks for the dream the other night," I said to him.

"You're welcome," he replied.

"How's everyone on the island? I sure miss them." I was fighting back tears.

"Everyone is good. And they know you miss them, and they miss you also." Willy had a calming way about him today.

"How long can you stay with me?" I asked.

"Not long. My trips back here are becoming shorter and shorter," Willy replied.

"Where do you go? What's it like?" I was curious now.

"There are no words in the human language that explain it," Willy said.

"What about...Is it good? Or is it bad?" Now I really wanted to know.

"Well, I guess it depends on how you get there. All I can say... Where I go is good. But I really can't explain it. But don't you get any ideas. It isn't your time yet. Now, I have to go. See you later." And with that, Willy was gone.

It didn't seem like Willy was with me that long or that I'd been walking that long or that far. The sun was going down, and I had a good ways to go before I got back to Bobby's house. By the time I returned, it was dark. The porch light was on, but one of the cars was gone.

I walked into the house, and there was a note from Bobby: *Gone to Sue's parents' house to tell them about the baby. Be back soon. Have some chicken; there is plenty in the refrigerator. Help yourself.*

I read the note and set it aside. Then I fixed myself a sandwich and a glass of milk and headed to my room. In there, I noticed a new crib, still in the box, standing in the corner. I guessed this was going to be the baby's room.

I opened the curtains and window so I could lie back and look at the stars. I wondered if the skies were the same everywhere. As I looked at the stars, I wondered about the people on Edisto. Boy, did I miss them. I wondered if they were looking at the same sky.

***

I must have wondered myself to sleep because the next thing I knew it was morning.

Bobby was knocking on the door saying, "You have that appointment this morning, so up and at 'em, my friend. We have to drop Carol off at school, so we have to leave soon."

"OK, I'll be ready in just a minute." Not realizing I had fallen asleep, I jumped out of bed, took a shower, and got dressed. I went into the kitchen to find Carol and Bobby ready to go.

Bobby handed me a piece of toast and said, "We got to go. Don't worry; we all were running late this morning. You ready for this, Scout?"

"Yes, ready as I'll ever be. Let's go," I said reluctantly.

As we were getting into the car, Bobby held the door for Carol to get in the back seat.

"Will I ever be old enough to sit in the front? Will I always sit in the back and look at the back of heads—never having a clear look out the front. Will I ever get to sit in the front?" Carol was laying it on thick.

"Stop being so dramatic, Carol. Just think: when this brother or sister of yours gets to where he or she can talk and ask you that question, what are you going to tell them? Because you will be in the front seat by then."

Bobby added, "Heck, you may even be driving by then, and then you'll know why you had to sit in the back." He was smiling at her at that point. Carol had nothing else to say.

The rest of the trip to her school was pretty quiet. When we got there, Carol gave Bobby a kiss on the cheek, jumped out of the car, and headed to the school's front door. She looked back with a big smile and waved goodbye.

When we got to the social services office, we were early.

Bobby said, "Scout, can you go in there and tell them who you are and that you have an appointment with them? They should be expecting you. If there are any problems, give me a call. I've got to get to the station. With all the doctor appointments, taking Carol, and Lieutenant Glen out, it's been crazy. So can you handle this by yourself?"

"Sure. And I'll call you when we're done." I was trying to be as calm as I could be, but I was scared to death. I got out of the car and walked a little before I started to cry.

By the time I got into the building, I had my composure back. I walked up to the front desk and said, "Hi. My name's Scout. I have an appointment here today."

The lady behind the desk said, "What is your last name, child?"

"Stevens," I said. "Go sit over there. Someone will be with you in a minute." I looked over to where she told me to sit, but there wasn't an empty seat anywhere. So I just went and stood in the corner, out of the way.

About an hour later, someone called my name. I walked over just to answer some questions: my address, why I was here, had I been to school. Then they told me to go sit down again. And, as before, no seats. So I went back to my corner.

Another hour went by, and they called my name again. This time I was directed to a tiny room, where there was only room for a desk and two chairs. There was a young lady behind the desk. She had long, dark hair and pretty green eyes. I thought I could like her. She said, "Sit down. It's already been a long day." It was a cold, uncaring voice. Her whole look changed. When I looked back at her, she was ugly. I did as I was told and sat down. I was ready to sit; I hated just standing.

"Have you had any kind of schooling since you ran away?" this lady said.

"Yes, I have," I answered her.

"Well, take this and go back out there and fill what you can out. Then let the lady at the front desk know when you're done. What you don't know just leave blank." With that, she handed me a stack of papers and a pencil, and back out to my corner I went.

It took me about another hour to finish what she had given me. When I walked up to the desk, there was a sign: *Gone to lunch. Be back at one.*

I thought, Good—all these people here will go to lunch, and I can have a seat.

Wrong. Everyone brought their lunches. These people must have gone through this a lot; they were prepared. A sign on the door said, *No eating or drinking.* But I guess, with everyone gone to lunch, it didn't matter. So I went back to my corner. I didn't have any money to go get anything.

There was a lady sitting down with two children. She'd been there all morning also. She gave me an apple. I was glad to get it, and I thanked her.

After lunch and after everyone was back at work, I took my paperwork up to the lady at the desk. She took it and said to go sit down. I

157

felt like a dog at obedience school. By now some of the people were clearing out. They must just make morning appointments because it takes them all day to deal with it. So now I could have a seat.

It was another hour before they called my name. I went back to that lady I saw before. Again, she looked like a nice lady till she opened her mouth. "You filled all this out by yourself?" She was giving me a nasty look.

"Yes, who else would fill it out?" I asked.

"Are you here alone?" she asked with a hateful look. Then she continued before letting me answer. "Why did you run away?"

"I didn't run away." She was getting on my nerves.

"Your parents said you ran away. Where did you go to school?" She was giving me a cold look.

"I had to go stay at a place to be safe, and the people there home-schooled me," I told her.

"Well, that's not the story your parents tell, but you did very well on this evaluation paper I gave you. You have the highest score I've ever gotten. And you did this all by yourself?" She was starting to ease up a little.

"Yes, ma'am. I did it by myself."

"Do you have any problem with going back home?" she said.

"I have nowhere else to go. So, no, I have no problem with going back to my parents." "Do you have all your things with you?" she asked me.

"No, my things are still at Sergeant Carson's house. He told me to call him when I was done here," I said.

"Well, let's give him a call because I want you back at your house as soon as possible. Your parents are worried about you," she told me.

"Yeah, right," I said to myself and gave the lady Bobby's phone number.

"Please step out while I talk to him, and I'll let him know he can come pick you up." She pointed to the door.

Back in the waiting room, there were plenty of seats by this time, so I sat down.

Bobby showed up a short time later. "The lady said you were a pretty smart kid, Scout. I told her I always knew that," Bobby said to me after I got into his car. "I have to take you to your parents tomorrow. Are you OK with that? You know you can call me at any time, and I'll be there for you. You know that, right?" Bobby wanted me to know he wasn't just getting rid of me.

"Yes. It's all good. I know I have to go back. It's OK. I'll be all right," I assured him, knowing I would have hell to pay when I got back to that house. We stopped and had a late lunch. Bobby said he hadn't eaten either. I was glad; that way, I could go for a walk when I got back—and not have to deal with anyone.

Later that evening, Bobby called Jessie. "Can you take Scout to her parents' house in the morning? I'm so far behind at work, and I have to get some things done." Jessie must have said yes because Bobby said, "She'll be ready by then. I'm sure. Thank you." Bobby walked into my room and said, "Jessie and Mae will be here around nine in the morning to take you to your parents. Are you sure you're all right with this?"

I told him, "Yes. It will be fine, and I'll be ready." It had been a long day, so I went to bed early.

Chapter 19

WELCOME BACK

The sun finally came up the next morning. Needless to say, I didn't get much sleep. I heard Bobby coming down the hallway and stop at Carol's room. He opened her door and said, "Get up, Carol. Let's go." Then he knocked on my door. "Scout, Jessie will be here soon. Time to get a move on."

I said, "OK." Then I heard Sue coming down the hallway.

"Bobby, I can take Carol to school today. I feel much better, and I have some things I need to do."

"OK. That would help me out," Bobby replied.

I was gathering my few things together when I heard Sue tell Carol, "Come on. We can grab some breakfast on the way." I thought, Boy, these people would die without fast food. By the time I was out of the room, everyone was gone.

Bobby left a note on the table: *Scout, if you need anything, please call me.*

There was a knock on the front door. Then I heard it open, and Jessie walked in. "You ready for this, Scout?"

"No, not really. But I don't know what else to do. I wish I could just go back to the island. It felt like home there."

I had what little stuff I owned in a bag and was heading to the door."I wish there was something I could do, Scout. If there were some way to change this, I would do it. Maybe after Thanksgiving, Mae and I could pick you up and go back to that island for a visit. What you think?"

"I don't know what to think, Jessie. But thank you. We'll see." I wasn't happy at all about what I had to do. "Come on, Jessie. Let's get this over with, please." I began heading to the truck. "No need to talk about it anymore." I got into the truck and shut the door. Jessie got into the driver's side, and we headed to my parents.

Not much was said along the route. I just stared out the window, calling to Grandma in my head: Please come take me back home. I was hoping she would come to me, but she didn't.

"Would you like something to eat before you go back, Scout?" Jessie asked, feeling really guilty.

At first I wanted to say no, but then I realized this might have been the only time I got to eat today. So I said, "Yes." There usually wasn't much to eat at my parents' house. So I said, "Yes." My oldest brother had a car, so all three brothers hung out together. And my parents would go out to eat, so there was never much as far as food in the house. But that was the only good thought about going back there: most of the time, no one was around. When they were, it wasn't a good thing.

Jessie pulled into a little country restaurant. I was glad because at least wasn't fast food. We walked into the restaurant and sat down. The waitress walked over and asked what we wanted to drink and handed us menus. Everyone else in the place was staring at us, like we were going to rob the place.

"Why is everyone staring at us, Jessie?" It was weird.

"Look here, Scout. You see the world in a totally different way than most people do. These people here see a big Black man with a cute, little White girl sitting together at a table. And they don't like it. That is why it would be hard on everyone if you came to live with us." Jessie was getting a little nervous at this time also.

"I know, Jessie. But it's a shame people can't get along." I was sad.

The waitress walked back over with our drinks and said, "Don't let those boys over there bother you. It'll be OK. What would you like to eat? We have a breakfast special: buy one, get one free." She had a friendly smile. "Two eggs, potatoes, and bacon—and, of course, toast."

Jessie looked at me. "Sounds good. What do you think, Scout?"

"Works for me," I said. After a while, people weren't staring so much. The waitress brought out our breakfast, set it down, looked at me, and said, "You look familiar. You live around here? You're those mean brothers' little sister who ran away awhile back, aren't you? What are their names? The Stevens boys? I guess you were found. I'm sorry...because I know they were hard on you."

"I'm going back today." I glanced at Jessie, who just lost his appetite. "It's OK, Jessie. It's not that bad."

The waitress turned her attention to Jessie. "Just out of curiosity... How do you fit in this mess?"

"Well, it's not any of your business, but I was asked to take her home. She's been friends with my wife and me for a while now." Jessie wasn't happy. "Could we please eat now?" Jessie said.

"I'm sorry—didn't mean to be nosy. If you need anything, let me know." With that, the waitress walked off. Jessie and I ate our breakfast in silence.

We left the restaurant and headed on down the road. I gave Jessie the directions. We finally got to the neighborhood where my parents lived. It was a nice house—not a rich man's house but a nice house—in a good neighborhood. We pulled up into the driveway and stopped. Jessie and I both were lost for words.

My oldest brother walked out of the house with the other two following him as always. My oldest brother looked at me, then back at the other two and said, "Look who's here. It must be Miss Daisy and her driver. 'Driving Miss Daisy.' Get it?" He looked at his brothers, and they all started to laugh.

"Don't mind him, Jessie. He's just a jerk." I could see Jessie getting mad. I got out of the car and said to Jessie, "You better go, Jessie."

I knew if either one of my parents came out, they also would have something to say.

Well, too late. Here they came. Both of them.

"Well, it's about time you came home. Who is this bringing you here? Scout, you don't even care who you're seen with," my mother said. "I really don't want people seeing you at my house, so please get that truck and yourself out of here."

Jessie put the truck in reverse and drove off. He had tears in his eyes and kept saying to himself "What have I done? Why did we bring her back to this." By the time he got home and saw Mae, he just broke down. He told Mae what had happened and what awful people they were. He looked at Mae with tears in his eyes and said, "Our child will never go through anything like that. I promise you that." By this time both of them were crying their eyes out.

"What can we do?" Mae asked.

"I don't know, but I'll call Bobby in the morning and tell him of the event. I just hope that there's something we can do." Jessie and Mae sat on the couch. Jessie's arm was around Mae, and they held each other close.

**

I walked into the house and was heading to what used to be my bedroom.

"Stop right there, little Miss Daisy. We moved your room to the basement," my father said. And the boys were snickering. "Miss Daisy," they were saying.

My father continued, "You aren't running away again."

"But it's cold and damp down there. I don't want to sleep down there," I said, knowing it would do no good.

"You aren't running off again, and if the only way to keep you here is to lock you up, I guess that's what I'll do. These boys keep us in enough trouble with social services. Then you go and run away. I can only fix one problem at a time. So, you're staying in the basement. No phone calls. Nothing. Do you hear me, Missy?" My father pointed to the basement.

Down in the basement I went. The door slammed, and the lock clicked. At least they had a light down there, and he had installed a toilet and a sink—but no walls around it. It was just sitting in the corner. They had me a cot, some blankets, and a small plug-in heater. It was actually more than I expected.

Boy, am I glad I had something to eat earlier. I sat on the bed and heard the boys get in their car and my parents get in another. I figured that was what they'd do. Everyone left to go get something to eat. My parents don't like anything that the boys like to eat, and vice versa.

I sat on my bed and thought, This might not be so bad, as long as they don't leave me for days. Boy, that was a dreadful thought.

It wasn't till late that night that the boys came home. They had been drinking and smoking pot. They unlocked the basement door, only to harass me. "Miss Daisy, you down there? You want me to call your Black driver up? You sure made Mom and Dad proud when you showed up with a Black man—you stupid girl."

I didn't know which brother it was, but it didn't matter. I was ignoring all of them. I just wished I could get out of there. But it was too cold to live on the street. I couldn't go to Bobby's or Jessie's; they had done all they could do, and I didn't want them in trouble.

I looked through my herbal book, which Miss Winnie had given me, to see if there was some way to poison the boys. The world would be a much better place if they weren't in it.

***

Finally it was morning. The only way I could tell was by the clock and by people walking around upstairs. I closed my eyes just to shut them out a little longer. I heard the door unlock and my mother's voice. "You want a biscuit?"

"Yes, please," I answered.

"You can come up and get it," she replied.

I walked upstairs and sat down at the table. My mother gave me a glass of milk and a sausage biscuit. I looked out the glass door. It was a gloomy day, with clouds that looked like sleet or snow. Time would tell. The ground was frozen—kind of the way I felt inside.

After I ate the biscuit and drank the milk, I asked my mother, "Can I go take a shower?"

"Make it quick. I have things to do. I'm not going to worry about you," she said with a frown. After my shower, I was locked back in the basement. I had something to eat, and I was clean. There was no one home, so I lay back on my bed and fell asleep.

Chapter 20

THANKSGIVING

I woke up with someone tugging at my foot. I didn't want to open my eyes. I just knew it was one of my brothers trying to make trouble for me. "Go away," I said.

"Scout, I need to talk to you, so wake up." It was my father. "Everyone has plans for tomorrow. Your brothers are going to some friends' house and your mom and I are going out of town with some friends. So I don't know what to do with you."

"Can I go to some friends then, since no one will be here?" I asked, not knowing where I would go.

"No way. All you'll do is run away. You have to learn to obey us," he continued. "I'm not going through all this crap with social services again."

"The boys are what got social services involved. The neighbors called the police on *them*. I did nothing wrong." I was getting mad.

"Well I'll tell you one thing, young lady: you're staying in this base- ment till we get back in a few days. Your mother is fixing you a cooler with everything you'll need. The boys will be back in the evening, and they'll check on you. And that's the way it's going to be." My father got up, walked back up the stairs, and closed and locked the door.

The boys brought down the big cooler that my father had mentioned and set it down. Then my mother came down with bread, drinks, cups, and paper towels.

One of the boys said, "Look at it this way, Scout: it'll be like camping out but never seeing the stars." All the boys laughed, and even my mother had a smirk on her face, like she was trying not to laugh.

But all in all, this wasn't a bad place to be right now. It was cold outside, starting to sleet and snow. This wasn't the warmest place I could be, but it could be worse. I went through the cooler to see what I had. It was mostly peanut butter, jelly, ham, mayo, and some cold fried chicken—just my luck. I put everything where I wanted it and sat on the bed.

I was looking around at all the boxes down here. For lack of nothing else to do, I started going through them. It was all of the boys' things from the time they were born till now. I didn't see anything that had anything to do with me—not even a picture. Well, the good thing was that there were some clothes that fit me in some of the boxes. I knew the boys weren't going to let me wash clothes while our parents were gone. Heck, I bet they wouldn't even open the door to down here while my parents are gone. This *was* the worst place ever, no matter how hard I tried not to think that way. I gave up and lay back down on the bed.

I concentrated on Grandma. Maybe she could hear me. I thought about all we had done: the dolphins, the birds, the turtles. The island was amazing. It just seemed like a dream long ago. I was wondering if it had really happened. I didn't know anymore; all I knew was that I hated this place. After a while I went back to sleep. I was looking for Willy in my dream, but he never showed up.

I must not have slept long. I could hear everyone talking upstairs and walking around.

I was wondering if I was ever going to get out of this place. The walls were starting to close in on me. I could only sleep so long. I started to cry.

* * *

Mae and Jessie were getting ready for family for Thanksgiving. Jessie couldn't get the picture of Scout having to walk into that house out of his head. It was supposed to be a special occasion because of the baby coming and all, but Jessie felt like a traitor—like he gave up his best friend to the enemy. Mae wasn't feeling good about the situation either. She looked at Jessie and said, "Go call Bobby and see what he thinks."

"OK. I think I will." And Jessie headed for the house.

Jessie went into the house and fixed himself a glass of sweet iced tea. He sat down at the kitchen table and picked up his phone. He sat there and thought a minute on what he was going to tell Bobby and how he was going to say it. The man had been through a lot. Jessie finally dialed Bobby's number.

Bobby answered with "Hello, Jessie. How are you doing in your new home?"

"It's good." Before he could say anything else, Bobby continued, "Does Mae like the house? I haven't been to see it yet. We'll have to do that one day soon." Jessie found it odd that he didn't even ask about Scout.

"Yes. You need to come see our new place soon. We really like it here," Jessie said, just going along with the conversation.

It got really quiet for a minute. Jessie thought that maybe the connection was lost, but then Bobby said, "How was Scout when you took her home?"

"It wasn't good," Jessie told him.

"I was afraid of that. She's been on my mind all day. I sure worry about her. Do you think they'll hurt her?"

"Her brothers were pretty hard on her, but I don't know. Is there anything we can do? Like, go check on her?" Jessie asked.

"I will check. But it being the holidays with no proof anything is wrong, I bet we can't do anything till Monday. I will check on some things and let you know. Now, if she calls you for help, then we can run in like the cavalry. But she has to call and ask for it."

"What if she can't call?" Jessie was worried.

"Let me make some calls. Just let me know if you hear from her." Bobby sounded in control.

"OK. I will," Jessie said and hung up. He turned around. Mae was right there, and they hugged each other for a minute, not saying a word. Afterward, they went back to planning for the next day.

***

Bobby called Lieutenant Glen. "Lieutenant Glen, this is Bobby."

"Would you please call me *Adam*? I think we've been through enough that we can call each other by their first name." Lieutenant Glen answered. "OK, Adam. I'm a little concerned about Scout. Jessie said it wasn't a pleasant experience. We aren't sure what we can do about it." Bobby was almost in tears.

"Bobby, what can I do to help? Everyone you need is off till Monday. So what can I do to help?"

"Well," Bobby started, "I was wondering if you could talk to Vic to see if he thinks she's safe. Scout said that people like Vic were put here to help others. She called him an 'onlooker.' So, I was thinking, if he had that same connection with Scout, maybe he would at least know if she is OK or not. If she isn't, then we do something more. What do you think?"

Bobby had grown to admire Vic's talent. "Where did she get this notion of Vic being an 'onlooker'? What is an 'onlooker'?" Lieutenant Glen was curious.

"From that place where she was at," Jessie said. "It was an island. There's an old lady there who taught her all kinds of things. You know, she saved my wife with some kind of healing soup. Scout said this old lady homeschooled her. She took a test of some sort at the social services office, and the lady there said Scout was smart. So, anyway, that's where she told me about onlookers. They can see something that might or might not happen, but sooner or later it will. Scout said the reason they act a little odd is they have to be able to shut the future off. I don't know what any of this means, but I'd love Vic's opinion."

"I'll talk to Vic this evening and let you know what he says. Onlooker—nice, I like it," Lieutenant Glen said with a smile. He got up and walked very slowly to Vic's room. Walking was still hard to do. When he got to Vic's room, Vic was sitting in the corner, staring into space. "What are you doing, Vic?" Lieutenant Glen asked.

"Nothing." "What are you thinking about, Vic?" Lieutenant Glen knew he had to say Vic's name to get a response.

"Nothing." Vic was just staring.

Mary Beth came into the room. "What are you all doing?" she asked, with a smirk.

"I just need to talk to your brother about something," Lieutenant Glen said.

"Good luck with that conversation. He doesn't talk to anyone unless he has something to say. Hey, Vic. What's happening?" Mary Beth said with disgust.

Vic replied, "Nothing."

"Yeah, good luck with that conversation, Uncle Adam." With that, Mary Beth left the room.

Lieutenant Glen looked back into the room to see Vic just staring into space, and he knew Mary Beth was right. There was no way he was going to get Vic to talk to him. So he headed slowly to the kitchen to find Nancy.

When Lieutenant Glen got to the kitchen, he sat down at the table exhausted. Nancy was at the sink washing something. She turned around when she heard the plunk of her brother sitting down. "Well it's about time you got up and moved around, Big Brother. What got you up and going?" Nancy was smiling.

"Well, I need to talk to Vic about something. You know, you always bring him to me when he wants to tell me something...or after he looks at something for me. But I don't think I've ever tried just talking to him. How do you just talk to him or get him to interact in conversation?"

Lieutenant Glen felt a little ashamed of himself when he heard his own words: "I don't think I've ever tried just talking to him."

"Well, he's different than most, and it does take practice and time. Go tell him what you want him to hear. And wait. He'll come back at some point and answer you, but I don't know when that will be. He hears real good and understands things that you wouldn't believe. Let me fix you something to eat, and then just go tell or ask him what you want, and wait. But—I warn you—when he decides to talk, that's when you have to listen."

Nancy turned back around and started fixing him something to eat. She brought him a cup of coffee while he was just staring, trying to figure out how to talk to Vic. "Now you look like Vic. See; it's not easy trying to communicate differently from others and trying to find the words. Now you're in Vic's world."

Lieutenant Glen looked up at his sister in deep admiration. "You are a good person, Sis."

After eating, Lieutenant Glen went back to his room and wrote down everything he wanted to ask Vic—like a police report. He had given Vic police reports before, to look at and get his vision on what he thought was going on. Most of the time, the boy was right or never responded. So Lieutenant Glen wrote his report and took it to Vic. "Vic, would you look at this and tell me what you think?"

He laid the report down and walked out of the room. When he looked back, he saw Vic pick it up.

* * *

I had been crying long enough. I picked up the book Grandma had given me. When I opened it, there was a note inside from Frankie. I had looked in this book from front to back many times, but there was never any note. I opened it slowly. I could hear people talking upstairs, and it sounded like the boys had some friends over. It was getting pretty loud. Maybe the police would come and find me. I hoped the neighbors would call the police. It was the only hope I had.

I opened the note, and it said, *Can't wait to see you on Thanksgiving, Love Frankie and Jim.*

Where did this come from? I asked myself over and over again. I held the note to my chest, wishing it were true. Then I heard music playing—but not the kind my brothers would listen to. I listened harder. It sounded familiar. I sat there straining my ears. Maybe I was dreaming? I didn't think I was dreaming. Then it dawned on me: that song was by John Prine, my favorite song "Angel from Montgomery." Oh, how I missed everyone on the island. What a cruel trick this was.

Then the door unlocked. Now what? I thought. I waited to see who was coming down the stairs. It was getting cold down here, so I was hoping that they were going to let me come up for a while.

Then I saw Willy. "Willy, what are you doing here? Am I dreaming?"

Then I saw Tommy and John. "How did you guys get here? Did they not stop you upstairs or anything? This must be a dream." I couldn't believe my eyes. I didn't care if it were a dream; I was liking it.

"No, this is not a dream," Tommy said. "John and I have come to bring you home. You've done what you were sent here to do, and now we're taking you home. And Willy here decided to come along."

"You can see Willy?" I asked.

"No. But he makes a big presence when he is around. I feel him and can hear him but can't see him. Only you can see him."

I looked at Willy, and he had a big smile on his face as he said, "We're taking you home."

"How did you get past my brothers upstairs? I think my parents are upstairs also. How did you get past everyone?" I was looking at Tommy and John.

John said, "It's OK, Scout. We got this. No worries. And you'll understand more when we get home. Are you ready?"

"Yes, of course I'm ready. But can I ask one thing before we go?" I was getting excited.

"What is it, Scout?" Tommy asked.

"What was my purpose for coming back?" I had to know.

"To save Sue Carson. You're a healer, and Grandma wanted you to prove it to yourself. It wasn't time for Sue to die, but if you hadn't come back, she would have," Tommy said with pride.

"You did a good job. Sorry it took so long to come back to get you. It's all about timing," John said with a smile.

"How do we get out of here? My whole family and half the neighborhood are upstairs." I was worried.

"It will be fine. Just follow us," Willy said, all proud of himself.

"OK. Whatever you guys say. Let's get out of here." I couldn't wait.

I grabbed my coat and the book that Grandma gave me, and I was ready. "Let's go. I'm following you. I'm going to be really mad if this is a dream and you get me beat up."

"You'll be fine, and it's not a dream," Tommy said as they were heading up the stairs.

Well, OK. Here we go, I thought.

Tommy and John walked up the steps and out into the house, like it was nothing. I was right behind them. People were sitting everywhere and talking, watching TV, eating popcorn—but never looked up. We walked straight past everyone while John was making faces and knocking over glasses of drinks. No one could see us. This had to be a dream. I hoped it never ended. It was getting late in the evening. It looked really cold, but I wasn't cold at all. We walked out the front door into the night air and never looked back.

***

Later that night, Vic walked into Lieutenant Glen's room and said, "Adam, wake up. Adam."

"What is it Vic? It's two in the morning."

"Adam, the girl is gone," Vic said, and he walked out of the room.

It took Lieutenant Glen a minute or two to get his thoughts together. What did that mean—the girl is gone? It was too late to rock the boat, so to speak. He would check first thing in the morning.

Lieutenant Glen didn't sleep the rest of the night, thinking Scout was dead or had run away. He knew that, first thing in the morning, he was going to find out. He finally fell asleep for what seemed like a minute, then Mary Beth walked into the room and said, "Mom said you have to get up. We have a lot to do today." Then she walked out.

Chapter 21

THE GIRL IS GONE

Lieutenant Glen got up very slowly and headed to the bathroom to bathe and get dressed. All he could think about was "The girl is gone." What did that mean? It just kept going over and over in his head. He finally got dressed and headed to the kitchen. Boy, was he stiff. Tossing and turning all night didn't make his body happy. He got to the kitchen, and Nancy gave him a cup of coffee.

"How was your night?" Nancy asked.

"Well, you were right about one thing: when Vic has something to say, he just comes right out and says it, no matter what time it is."

"I told you, Adam. When he come up with what he has to say, he'll let you know," Nancy said with a smile.

Vic walked into the kitchen and sat down at the table. "Good morning, Vic. How are you this morning? Look at me, Vic, and answer me, please," Nancy said firmly but not harsh.

Vic hesitated but looked at Nancy and replied, "Fine, thank you."

"Good job. Now, would you like breakfast, Vic?" Nancy asked.

"Cereal with milk. And orange juice, please," Vic said, like it was a script. Nancy served Vic and walked away to start the turkey.

"Vic, what did you mean last night when you said 'The girl is gone'?" Lieutenant Glen figured this was as good a time as any to ask.

Vic replied, "The girl is gone. That is all." Lieutenant Glen knew that Vic had nothing else to say.

"What girl?" Nancy asked.

"The girl who was with Bobby Carson when he came by the other day. Bobby said he saw you at the door leaving when he came in," Lieutenant Glen answered.

"Girl? There was no girl with Bobby when he came here the other day. Vic and I met him at the door, and he was alone," Nancy said confused.

"Maybe she hadn't gotten out of the car yet, but Scout was with Bobby. You've heard me talk about that little girl, Scout, I know. She was the child who got all involved with the case where those horses were stolen. The trial comes up in two weeks," Lieutenant Glen said.

Mary Beth walked in with an ornery look, sat down, looked at Nancy, and said, "I want something to eat."

"*Please*," Nancy said quickly. "I'm tired of this attitude, Mary Beth. You better get over it, at least for today. Do you understand me?" Nancy wasn't in the mood for nonsense today.

Lieutenant Glen thought this would be a good time to break into the conversation before it got ugly. "Mary Beth, you saw Scout with Sergeant Carson the other day, didn't you? You walked into the room when we were talking. Do you remember?"

"No, sir. I didn't see any girl with Sergeant Whoever."

"Go to your room!" Nancy scolded her. Mary Beth headed out of the kitchen and down the hallway.

Nancy looked at her brother and said, "You would think Vic would be the problem child." Then she went back to cooking.

Lieutenant Glen left the kitchen and went back into his room to call Bobby, who answered his phone on the first ring.

"Good morning, Lieutenant Glen." Bobby knew it was him. "Did you find out anything about Scout?"

Lieutenant Glen replied, "Not really. Does anyone in your house remember Scout? I know that sounds odd, but no one here remembered seeing her with you the other day. And all I get out of Vic is 'The girl is gone.' What does that mean? I think you need to send a car out there to check on her. While you're at it, could you have one of the officers bring me the police reports on the Hunter case? The trial is three weeks away, and I don't want anything to go wrong. And last but not least, Happy Thanksgiving."

Lieutenant Glen seemed frazzled. Something didn't feel right. Bobby was thinking maybe Lieutenant Glen was losing it. Everyone saw Scout at his house the other day. "Yes, I'll send a car out to check on Scout. Are you sure no one remembers Scout with me the other day? We spoke to everyone...or I did. Scout didn't say anything, I don't think. I know she spoke to you and me. That's crazy. But now that I think about it...I said something to Sue about Scout, and she said, 'Who?' Then the phone rang or something, and it wasn't brought up again. And she hasn't been talked about at all. Does seem strange... I'll have those reports brought out to you also. I'll let you know about Scout as soon as I do. Oh, and thank you and Happy Thanksgiving to you and your family."

Lieutenant Glen replied, "Thank you, we'll talk soon." Then they both hung up.

Sue was standing behind Bobby when he hung up the phone. "Does that man ever give you a day off? Do you have to go down to the station?"

Bobby was shocked. He didn't know she was behind him. "Actually, I called him yesterday and asked him for a favor. Speaking of that, do you remember Scout staying here for about a week or so? She made you soup that healed you."

"I don't have time for your games. I have a dinner to fix." Sue walked off back into the kitchen.

"Sue, I'm not playing games. Do you remember the little girl Scout?" Bobby followed her into the kitchen.

"I don't know who you're talking about, Bobby. Really, what is this all about?" Sue stopped, turned around, and looked at Bobby. He continued, "She stayed in the spare room. She was here for over a week. She cleaned the house and cooked food for us." Bobby followed Sue to the spare room as Carol came down the hallway. "Carol, you remember Scout, don't you? She stayed here and cooked so we didn't have to eat chicken anymore. You remember, right?" Bobby felt like he was losing it.

"Sorry, Dad, but I thought Mae did all that. I don't remember anyone staying here." Carol could tell her dad was getting upset.

Bobby went to the room that Scout had stayed in and opened the door to look inside. To his surprise, he saw a nursery—a crib, the walls painted, the whole nine yards. "When did this happen? Who did this?" Bobby now was on the verge of a breakdown.

"I had it done this week. They just finished it yesterday. I wanted to surprise you. We were working on it when you weren't here. Are you mad?" Sue was starting to cry.

Bobby put his arm around her and said, "No, I'm not mad, just a little confused. I need to go to the station, but I'll be back in time for dinner. What time does everyone get here?"

"They'll start getting here around eleven. So please don't be late. Your parents and my parents both will be here plus my sister." Sue was calming down, and so was Bobby.

"OK, I promise I'll be here."

✳✳✳

Bobby went to the station and told one of the officers on duty to check on a little girl. He handed him a piece of paper with the address. He told the officer to be sure and call him when he got there and tell him how she was. The young officer said he would and walked out of the building.

Then Bobby walked into Lieutenant Glen's office to get the police reports he wanted. He figured he would take them to him so he could tell him about what had happened at his house. No one remembered Scout. That was strange. He picked up the reports. Thumbing through them, he couldn't believe what he saw. He gathered all the papers to the reports and left and headed to see Lieutenant Glen.

When he got to Nancy's house guests were already arriving. Bobby knocked on the door, and Mary Beth answered.

"Oh, it's you again. I guess you want to see Uncle Adam, right? That invisible girl is not with you, is she?" Mary Beth looked behind Bobby.

"No. Can I come in and see your uncle, please? I have some papers he wanted to look at." Bobby wasn't liking this little girl much.

"Come in. He's in his room. Do you not have a family to have Thanksgiving with? Do you not know this is Thanksgiving Day?" said Mary Beth, her bossy self.

"Yes, I know what day it is. And yes, I have a family, and I won't be long." Bobby just made his way past her and headed to Lieutenant Glen's room.

He walked in. Lieutenant Glen was sitting in a chair looking like he didn't want to be there. He looked at Bobby and said, "I didn't mean for you to bring me those reports, Bobby. You get on back to your family."

"I will. I just wanted to bring this to you. I think you're going to find it very interesting when you read it. I sent an officer to check on Scout. I should hear from him any minute now." Bobby no sooner said it than his phone rang. He answered it. "Really?...OK...No...I know no one is home. Then that is all I needed to know. Thank you." Bobby hung up. "That was the officer I sent over to check on Scout. He said no one was home, and no cars are in the driveway. They must have gone somewhere for Thanksgiving. We can't enter the house without cause. What do you think we should do, Lieutenant Glen?" Bobby didn't like it. Something wasn't right.

"Bobby, we may have to wait this one out a little longer. Check with social services on Monday, and go from there." Lieutenant Glen didn't like it either, but their hands were tied. There was nothing they could do right now. "Bobby, go home and have a good Thanksgiving.

We'll deal with this later." Lieutenant Glen could hear the people in the other room.

Bobby said, "OK. But one last note: no one in my house remembers Scout even being there." That put cold chills up Lieutenant Glen's neck and Bobby's neck also when he heard himself say it. "Wait till you look at that report. Something strange is going on." Bobby turned, headed for the door, and said, "Have a good Thanksgiving."

Lieutenant Glen picked up the report and thumbed through it when Nancy came to the door. "Come on, Adam. We have guests, and they want to see you. Now put down those papers, and let's go." He got up slowly and headed out to see the guests. And there were a lot of them. Most he didn't recognize, but some he did, and all of them seemed to know him.

***

Bobby returned to a house full of people also. When he walked in the door, Sue greeted him with a frown. "Jessie called. He wanted you to call him back." With that, Sue walked away. Bobby knew she was upset, and he would deal with that as soon as he called Jessie.

Jessie's phone only rang once. "How is Scout?" Jessie asked without even saying hello.

"No one was home when I sent a car out there. I hope she went somewhere with her family," Bobby replied.

"I wouldn't think so...but maybe. Well, we have a crowd here, and I know you do too—so Happy Thanksgiving to you and your family, and we'll talk soon. I know I'll be praying that Scout is OK," Jessie said.

"Happy Thanksgiving to you and your family, and we'll talk tomorrow." With that, Bobby and Jessie hung up the phone.

Sue walked up to Bobby and said, "Are you working today?"

Bobby said, "No." "Are you going to see your family in the other room? It's about time to eat." "Yes, I'm done with anything to do with work today. I'm all yours." And with a smile, Bobby said, "Beat me if you must; I've been a bad boy."

Sue couldn't help but laugh and say, "Come on, bad boy. Let's go eat—and the discipline will come later." Then Sue wrapped her arm around Bobby's arm, and they walked into the dining room, where all the guests were.

Jessie went into the kitchen, where Mae was getting food ready to take out to their guests, and told her what Bobby had said about Scout.

She replied, "Well, let's just hope she's all right because we cannot do anything but pray for her at this time. But, Jessie, I feel deep in my bones that she is all right. I don't know how to explain it." Jessie could tell she wasn't just saying that to make him feel better; she really meant it.

"Well, Mae, that does make me feel better. So let's go feed the family." Jessie patted Mae on the belly and said, "Let's go eat, my little man." Mae couldn't help but smile. Each of them grabbed some food and took it into the dining room.

Chapter 22

THE POLICE REPORT

After all the food and people, Lieutenant Glen was exhausted. He lay down on his bed and picked up the police report that Bobby had brought him. That was the last he remembered; he fell fast asleep.

When he woke, it was about three o'clock in the morning. The police report still on his chest, he made a little chuckle, "I've not passed out like that since I quit drinking." He picked up the report and started reading. Then he started flipping through the pages like he was searching for something. This can't be all of the report, he thought. Then he remembered what Bobby had said, "Wait till you look at that report. Something strange is going on." He didn't think much about then. This couldn't be right; something was wrong. He couldn't call anyone; it was 3:00 a.m. So he picked up the report and started reading from the beginning. This couldn't be right. He began reading out loud, as if that would change anything. The report started...*Jessie McVeigh reported seeing three men stealing horses out of the back pasture at the Hunter farm. Horses were also reported stolen at the farm next door to the Hunters. (See report number 10045.) When the investigation started, there were approximately thirty horses stolen.*

This wasn't right. Where was the boy who was shot? Mae called it in, but Scout saw the boy getting shot. But none of this was even mentioned.

Lieutenant Glen read further into the report and realized that nothing was said about Gary either. Everything else was in there: the load of horses killed in the wreck, but no Gary; the young officer who was shot and what had happened to him.

Mr. Hunter and his crew are still going to jail, he thought. And I like that Scout and Gary won't have to come to court. But it's so odd that they aren't in the report.

Lieutenant Glen finally fell back asleep. He was still weak from his wounds.

***

Bobby was up and dressed before the sun came up. As he was walking out the door, the sun was just coming up. It was a cold, crisp morning, and the frost was heavy on the ground, with big patches of snow. Winter was on her way. Bobby was slipping and sliding on his way to the car. There will be lots of accidents today, he thought. He drove up to the station and got out of his car. A young officer waved and said, "Hope you had a good Thanksgiving, Sergeant Carson."

"I did. Thank you," Bobby replied. He went into the office and picked up the reports from the day before to catch up on what was going on.

Another officer stuck his head into Bobby's office and said, "It was a quiet day yesterday, considering it was Thanksgiving. Some domestic violence and a traffic ticket or two—and that was it."

"That's good to hear. I think we've had enough violence for a while." Bobby continued, "Do you remember a little girl living in Mr. Hunter's barn when all that horse stealing was going on?"

"No, sir. I was on vacation when all that was happening. I missed the biggest criminal event we've ever had in this town. But that's OK. I sure miss Officer Franks; he was a good friend of mine. I should have been here for him." The young officer looked sad.

"I wish I'd been there for him too," Bobby said. He looked at the young officer. "We all do the best we can."

"Yes, sir. We do." With that, the young officer headed out to his patrol car.

Bobby looked through the reports, got up, and headed out the door. He told the girl in the office he was heading over to the social services office if anyone needed him. He got in his car and called Lieutenant Glen, who answered, "Good morning, Bobby. How are things this morning?"

"Good, good. I'm heading over to the social services office to see if we can get into the house to check on Scout. What did you think about the police report on the Hunter case?" Bobby had skimmed over the reports and saw that Scout wasn't mentioned, nor was the boy." Something strange was going on.

"Come by here when you have time. We need to talk, and I need to go back to my house, where I can get some rest. So if you have a minute, I would love a ride. If I get bossed around by this little girl here any longer, I may end up in jail." Lieutenant Glen sounded drained."

"OK, I'll come by as soon as I get done with social services and Scout. I'll call you when I'm on the way," Bobby told him. With that, they hung up.

Bobby walked into social services and asked for the files on Scout Stevens. The lady behind the desk said, "I'm sorry, sir, but no one by that name has been in here, nor have I had an appointment for such a person. Maybe you are mistaken?"

"No, ma'am, I'm not. I brought her here; I made the appointment. Are you sure you don't have a report on her?"

Bobby didn't want to sound too upset, but this whole thing had been too weird. "I'm sorry, sir. I have nothing," the lady behind the desk said.

"OK. Well, thank you for your time." Bobby walked out the door. He headed for Scout's parents' house. When he got there, he saw her brothers and some friends hanging out in the driveway. He stopped, and the boys were ready to run. They all looked like villains.

Bobby rolled down the window and said, "Hey! Just checking to see how Scout is."

"Who?" one of the brothers said, as he walked over to the car.

"Your sister, Scout. A Black man brought her home last Tuesday," Bobby replied.

"Sir, we don't have a sister. We've never had a sister—don't want a sister," the one brother told him. By now all the boys were beside the car.

"Where are your parents?" Bobby asked.

"They are out of town and won't be back for a couple of days," one of the other brothers said.

"And you're telling me you don't have a sister?" Bobby asked again.

"No, sir. This is probably the only truth I will tell today," one of the brothers said, and the rest just laughed and walked away.

Bobby left and went to go pick up Lieutenant Glen. When he got to Nancy's house, he knocked on the door.

Mary Beth answered. "Oh, it's you again. Do you live here now? Uncle Adam is in his room, packing, and Mom is not happy. So there." With that, she walked away.

Bobby walked in and went to Lieutenant Glen's room to see him packed and ready to go. "Hello, Lieutenant. How are you feeling?" Bobby asked.

"I'll feel better when I get to my house. This house is too busy for me. What did you find out about Scout?" Lieutenant Glen was tired. He had been packing and arguing with Nancy all morning. She wanted him to stay a little longer.

"Nothing," Bobby continued. "You, Jessie, Mae, and I are the only people I know who even know she exists. I've been to social services and her house, and everyone looks at me like I'm crazy."

Lieutenant Glen said, "Well, evidently, that Willy boy and the horse trainer, Gary, never existed either. I called the hospital to get

185

his medical records, and they told me he was never there. I did call the district attorney's office, and they said that the case was solid, so I didn't want to rock the boat with any odd questions—if you know what I mean."

Lieutenant Glen picked up his bags, looked at Bobby, and said, "Let's get out of here while we have a chance. That little monster child might come back in here and start fussing." With that, they grabbed everything, headed out the front door, got into the car, and left.

As they drove, Lieutenant Glen looked at Bobby and said, "What do you think happened to those people, Bobby? I know what I know—and I know those people were here."

Chapter 23

AND THE SEARCH GOES ON

The trial went over without a hitch. Mr. Hunter was found guilty of murder and a list of other things. He got life without parole. The lawyer got fifteen to twenty, and the others got twenty-five to life. Nothing was ever mentioned about Scout, Gary, or the boy who was killed. The four of us thought about them every day—what a strange thing.

One evening, Bobby invited Jessie, Mae, and Lieutenant Glen over to talk about what had happened. Bobby had told Sue the story of Scout staying with them and fixing the soup so many times that it must have been true. However, Sue still couldn't believe the man she loved so dearly. So she asked Bobby to invite everyone over so she could hear everyone's side of the story. If nothing else, it would be a fascinating story when Bobby shared it with the others.

Everyone showed up that night for dinner at Bobby's house. Carol was spending the night with a friend. Sue had made barbeque chicken with potato salad and green beans. Everyone sat down at the table and fixed their plates. The food was good, and Lieutenant Glen especially loved it. After he moved back home, he ate no good food, just cans and takeout.

It was a little while before Sue asked Mae about the soup. "Who made the soup when I was sick, Mae?" Somebody had to break the ice. Mae looked at Bobby because it had almost become taboo to even talk about it. Everyone felt crazy or something.

Bobby could see the confusion in Mae's face. "It's OK," Bobby said. "I've told her the story many times; she just wants to hear it from you and everyone. And I think we need to talk about it because I don't want to forget Scout or the others. I think we were part of something very cool. So I think we need to talk about it."

Mae started first: "Yes, Sue. She made this soup for you after I had gone, but when she gave it (or anything she fixed) to you, she told you I made it. She said she didn't think you would eat it if she said she made it. I don't know what was in that soup, but it sure fixed you right up. She stayed here a week or close to it."

Sue replied, "That's what Bobby keeps saying. But he said I also met her when he took Carol and me down to the barn where you work. I don't remember that either. Why, Carol does not remember it either. That's what is so strange."

Jessie started next: "I was at the farm when you and little Carol came to visit. You even gave Scout a coat to wear to school. And, by the way, she still wears that coat."

"Why do I not know these things?" Sue was thinking she had lost her mind.

"Now calm down, Sue. You were the one who wanted to hear this. How do you think we feel when no one believes what we're saying?" Bobby was trying to calm her down.

Lieutenant Glen was next: "What a sweet girl. I don't think I ever saw her mad, no matter what we did to her. We sent her away. We brought her back. We sent her to the last place she wanted to be. And now she's gone. I just want her to be OK. It's really hard to talk about her. But what a sweet child she was. She loved that dog and those horses, and they loved her too."

Mae chimed in, "And she loved that island too. What a beautiful place it was. Those people loved that child, and she loved them. You don't reckon they came and took her back? The older lady there—she homeschooled Scout and taught her all kinds of things."

Bobby broke in, "Do you know that the lady at the social services office said Scout scored the highest on the placement test? The test to see what their grade level is. Anyway, she scored the highest ever. And then the next time I go there, they think I'm crazy because no one with that name had ever been there—"

"Tell me more about the island, Mae," Sue interrupted. She had heard all about what Bobby was going on about, but this was the first she had heard about the island.

"They called it Edisto, but I can't find anything on it. I've looked at maps...called around the area...but no one knows anything about it. It's so strange." Mae looked relieved to be able to talk about this and be believed.

Then Jessie started: "Yeah, Gary set it up for Scout to go to that island, and he was to keep it secret so no one could find Scout. Then Gary needed to go home to heal from his wounds, so we took him home and picked up Scout. Both of them now...no one has ever even heard of them, and it's like they vanished into thin air."

Mae began: "The island was like floating on a cloud. I don't know how to explain it. It is a wondrous place. I would love to go back there again."

"Now that sounds like a grand idea," Sue said. "Then we can put all this to rest. When do you want to go?" Sue was all excited.

Lieutenant Glen said, "No way can I ride for that long in a car yet. I get stiff sitting here. Boy, I hope no one ever shoots me again; this is not fun."

"Jessie, do you remember how to get there?" Sue said, getting all involved in this.

"Yes, I do. I still have the directions for most of the way. For the last little bit, Gary told me the way, but I think I can find it." Jessie was just glad someone else believed the story.

"I have next weekend off," Bobby said next.

"Carol can stay with her grandparents," Sue continued.

"Jessie?" Mae was looking at Jessie. "What do you think? Can we do it next weekend?" Mae was feeling the excitement.

"Now, if we find Scout and she wants to stay—and I know she will—we aren't forcing her back here just to prove a point, are we? Because if we are, I want no part of it. I took that child away from there once and put her through hell; I won't do it again." Jessie felt so guilty bringing her back here not knowing Scout was meant to come back.

"We all agree that, when we find Scout, she can do whatever she wants," Bobby said. And everyone agreed.

Sue filled in, "It looks like she can do whatever she wants anyway. This is going to be fun—off to an island no one has even heard of." Sue could hardly stand it. She was so excited. "OK. Next weekend it is. We can get a hotel room on the way. This, I hope, is going to be a nice getaway, a little adventure." Bobby was getting a little excited too.

Everyone was eating and talking all about Scout, Gary, and Willy. Sue was hanging on every word—the fact that these three people just vanished off the face of the earth.

During the conversation, Sue asked, "Who picked up Scout and brought her to the island?"

Mae looked at Jessie and said, "You were there, Jessie. I don't think you ever told me who picked her up. Was it a man or woman?"

"You know, I remember Gary being there and the two horses loaded, but I can't for the life of me remember who took her. Never even thought about it till just now." Jessie looked puzzled. "I remember the day, and I remember Gary. But I don't remember anything else but Scout being gone. Strange I tell you—something strange is going on."

After dinner everyone got their coats and felt a little relieved. They were able to talk about everything without feeling foolish. Plans were made for the next weekend, and everyone said good night.

Sue looked at Bobby and said, "It *was* a good night." Bobby agreed, and they headed for bed.

Sue tossed and turned all night, thinking about the island with people no one remembers. She couldn't wait till next weekend. This is going to be the longest week ever, she thought.

The following weekend came quicker than Bobby expected. They were leaving early in the morning. Sue was ready before daylight. Jessie and Mae showed up shortly after. Bobby, Jessie, and Mae weren't has excited as Sue. Something was different this morning, and they all felt it. It wasn't a bad feeling or a good one; it was just different. It was a cold and cloudy morning, and it looked like it might snow. The weatherman said there'd be no snow today. But what do they know? They never look outside.

Bobby packed the car with things they may need. Sue had packed everyone a lunch, and Mae brought the water and tea. Everyone was loaded, and the car drove off before 7:00 a.m. As they drove along, Sue would ask questions, and they would be answered, but not much else was said.

"What is wrong, people? This is supposed to be fun. Why all the long faces?" Sue was trying to make a fun trip out of this.

"OK, OK," Bobby said. "We could stop and see some of the sights along the way. What do you all think?" He was trying to accommodate Sue so she would be quiet.

Jessie reluctantly said, "Well, you know, there's this old horse farm they turned into a winery, up the road a ways. We could stop and eat lunch there. It's a real pretty place."

"That's a real nice place. It would be a good stop for lunch," Mae said. And everyone agreed.

When they got to the winery, it started to rain a little. "I bet it will be snowing at the house tonight. If these clouds head toward the house, being as cold as it is, it will surely snow." Bobby was just trying to make conversation.

"Yes, it probably will," Jessie said.

Mae broke in: "Come on, guys. They have a place inside where we can eat, taste a little wine, and then tour the place. It won't take long, and it's worth it."

Sue was all for that. So they grabbed their baskets and cooler and headed inside.

It was a beautiful place. They walked inside, and the tables had white tablecloths, with a candle in the middle. There were different size tables, and the lady at the door said, "Sit anywhere." The travelers were the first there or maybe the only ones. They picked a table, sat down, and started unpacking their lunch. They could order food here, but Sue had packed a good lunch. The waitress came by with some water and three small glasses of three different types of wine for everyone to taste. Sue found one she really liked and bought two bottles of it. She drank most of one bottle before they left. They took the tour, bought some wine, and got back in the car.

Sue fortunately had enough wine to put her to sleep. The minute she got into the car and got comfortable, she was out like a light. "The winery was a great idea, Jessie," Bobby said with a grin on his face. Jessie and Mae both smiled in agreement. No other words were spoken.

Jessie was driving when they came across a cute little motel. It sat by a big pond. Jessie pulled in. "Bobby, I think this will be a nice place to stay tonight. The turnoff to get to the island is about twenty miles down the road, and I don't think there will be anywhere else to stay. I don't recall seeing this place when we were here before."

"We weren't looking for a place to stay last time," Mae said.

"That's true. But what a cute place! You would have thought we would have noticed," Jessie replied.

Sue woke up, and they all got out and walked into the motel. They reserved two rooms and unloaded their things. It was early in the evening, so Jessie suggested, "Let's go see what we can find to eat, and after I want to go find that turnoff to the island so in the morning we can go straight there. What do you all think?"

"Sounds like a plan to me," Bobby said.

"I'm getting hungry too," Sue chimed in.

"Me too," Mae said.

They stopped at a nice little seafood restaurant, not far from the motel. On the menu, it had Edisto shrimp. Mae was so excited and asked the waitress, "Where is Edisto Island from here?"

The waitress just laughed. "There's no such place. We get our shrimp from the Edisto River. People have talked about an island, but I don't know anyone who has actually been there. Some people say that there is a voodoo witch who lives there. I've lived here all my life, and there is no island. Now, can I take your order?"

Everyone ordered the shrimp and iced tea. Nothing more was said about the island. Jessie and Mae knew firsthand that there was an island. Needless to say, the Edisto shrimp were wonderful.

After eating, they left to find the turnoff. It was dark now, and it was hard to see. Out in the low country, there were no lights on the road.

Jessie said, "That turnoff is right along here somewhere."

They came across a little country store that looked like it was still open. An old Black man walked out of the store and sat on the front porch.

Jessie got out first. "Hello, my name is Jessie. Can we ask you some questions, please?"

"Sure. Go inside. Get you something to drink. And come on out here and have a seat. It is a good night for a talk." The Black man sat in a chair and pointed inside, for everyone to get what they wanted to drink. And after they did, they all came out and sat down. What a beautiful night it was. You could see every star in the sky. At first, they just sat in awe of the view.

The Black man introduced himself. "Hello, everyone. My name is Joe. May I ask what brings you all here tonight?"

Jessie couldn't help himself, so he started. He told this old man all about Scout—who she was to them and how they sent her to this island for protection. They brought her back, and now she has vanished. And now no one remembered her but just four people. They were hoping that she made it back to the island. All they wanted to know she was OK. Jessie went on for a long time, telling everything he knew. He told him about Willy and Gary. He just couldn't stop till the whole story was told.

"So you and your beautiful wife got invited to go on Edisto?" the old man asked.

"Yes," Mae said, "and what a wonderful place it was."

"How did you know it was called Edisto?" Jessie asked. He had not said the name of the island.

"I know this place well," Joe said. "Only very special people get invited to go there, and very powerful people or children get to stay."

"Yes. Scout said something about healers, helpers, searchers, and onlookers. Do you know what she was talking about?" Bobby asked.

"Yes, I do," Joe said with pride.

"And since you remember her so well, she has left part of herself in all of you."

"I don't remember her at all, but they said she saved me with some kind of soup." Sue felt left out, and, really, she did not feel like she was even there.

"That must have been why Winnie let her go back with you. She wanted to test her. Boy, that healing soup is good," Joe said with a chuckle. "I see she did a good job." He looked at Sue and smiled. Joe continued, "Now, just sit back and know this little girl is OK, and listen to the drum beating in the distance."

"What drums?" Sue asked.

"Just sit back and close your eyes and listen, and you can hear the drums of Edisto."

Everyone sat back and laid their heads against the building and listened. Finally they could hear the drums in the distance. They sounded so far away...

"Mom, Dad, you going to sleep all day? Dad, Jessie is on the phone. He wants to talk to you. He said it was important. I told him you were still in bed." Carol was standing in the doorway of their bedroom.

Bobby was lost.

Sue looked at him and said, "Honey, you look like you've seen a ghost or something. Are you OK?"

Bobby got up and staggered to the phone. "Hello," Bobby said timidly.

"Do you know what day this is?" Jessie said, with scary excitement.

"No," Bobby said, trying to figure out how he got here. "This is Saturday. What happened to us? I know yesterday was Saturday, and we left to find the island. We stopped at that little country store. And now we're here, and it's Saturday again."

"OK," Bobby started. "Sue doesn't remember anything. Does Mae remember everything like we do?"

"Yes, but she says that all our questions were answered, and that is why we went. But that does not answered why this is Saturday." Jessie was so confused.

"Jessie, listen to me. Let's just ride this out and see what happens. I don't want people to think we are crazy. I feel crazy right now, but we're safe and we're home. Let it go for right now, please." Bobby just felt like that was the best thing.

"That's what Mae said, but I wanted to make sure it wasn't just that Mae and I were going crazy." Jessie said.

In the background, Mae said, "We aren't going crazy. Did you not listen to the old man. We are special, and one day maybe we can go back to Edisto."

Nothing else was ever mentioned about that day. It was too hard to believe and even harder to talk about.

Chapter 24

THE DAY HAS FINALLY COME

Sue and Mae had become very close friends over the summer—both of them getting bigger and bigger. But neither of them had been sick or uncomfortable through this whole time. Mae knew Scout was looking after them, but Sue had not a clue. Sue would talk about how sick she was the whole time she was pregnant with Carol. Carol was also looking forward to the new baby.

Life is good, Mae thought. Jessie had graduated from the police academy and was now working under Bobby. They, too, have become extra close over the summer. Mae was sitting in her kitchen just daydreaming. It was a beautiful morning: no humidity, and the sun was just coming up. She could see it through her picture window in the kitchen. She loved this house, and today she and Jessie would go sign the papers on it. The owners agreed to sell it, and, now that Jessie had a steady job, they were going to buy it. Mae couldn't wait. There would be a dinner party tonight. But then she went to get up, and the weight of the baby made her decide the dinner party could wait.

Jessie paced around the station waiting for two o'clock. That was when they had to be at the lawyer's office to sign the papers for the house.

Bobby walked in. "Jessie, what are you doing pacing around like that?"

"You know we are signing for the house today, right? I've never in my life borrowed that much money. My parents could never afford a house. They are proud of me though. But, Bobby, this is a big deal for me." Jessie was just a mess.

Bobby laughed. "It will be OK, my friend. I promise. Now, let's get some work done. Lieutenant Glen will be here shortly, and he wants the weekly reports on his desk. So come on. You have a lot to do before two o'clock. By the way, how is Mae taking all this?"

Jessie replied, "Like we have been buying houses all our lives. She said it was meant to be. 'And stop worrying.' Nothing bothers that woman." Jessie walked off to his space to look at the reports before putting them on Lieutenant Glen's desk.

Lieutenant Glen walked in just as Jessie was putting the reports on his desk. "How are you this morning, Jessie? I hear you are going to buy a house. Congratulations! This is a good day."

Bobby said, "I wouldn't go there, Lieutenant. He's so upset; he's likely to birth that baby for Mae." Bobby laughed and walked out the door to his car. He was glad for Jessie, who deserved having something go right. He had also become a good friend.

While Bobby was driving, he heard a call over the radio to an address that sounded familiar. It was some kind of disturbance at a house. Someone heard gunshots. One of the neighbors. Bobby turned on his blue lights and siren and headed to the address. I won't lose another officer, Bobby thought.

When he arrived, two other cars were already there. Bobby realized that this was Scout's parents' house. He could see one boy lying in the front yard. An officer was sitting next to him. Jessie was one of the cars that were there. He walked over to Bobby and said, "I knew this address. And these boys are nothing but trouble."

"What happened?" Bobby asked.

"The youngest boy got mad at his brothers, so he got a gun and started shooting. It was just a little .22 pistol, and he was a bad shot. He did shoot his two brothers—one in the arm, the other in the foot. I think they will live. An ambulance is on the way, and we are taking the youngest to juvenile lockup. There is someone from there coming to pick him up." Jessie needed this to distract him from the house buying.

Bobby looked at Jessie and said, "Did you get to look inside the house? Did you see anything that would have let you know if Scout was ever here?"

"You know, Bobby, I thought the same thing. So I did look around and saw nothing. But in the basement, where all this started, is a pool table and a toilet in the corner of the room—no walls around, nothing. I asked one of the boys about it, but he said he didn't know why his dad put it there. It just seemed odd to me. But they still say they never had a sister." Jessie had had Scout on his mind also. "Well, it looks like you all have this all under control. I'll see you later." With that, Bobby went and got in his car, just as the ambulance was pulling in. As Bobby was leaving, he thought, I wonder where the parents were this time. I'll be sure to read that report.

Later that evening, Sue had made dinner and asked Bobby and Carol to come eat. They were planted on the couch in front of the TV. Carol was snuggled up under her dad's arm. They reluctantly got up and headed for the kitchen. As they sat down to the good meal, Bobby asked Carol, "How was school today? You haven't said much about it. Everything OK?"

"Yes, everything is good," Carol started, "but I do have something to show you...if it's OK to show you now. I wanted you both together."

"What is it, Carol? You OK?" Sue asked, concerned something was wrong.

Carol slowly handed her mom a piece of folded paper. Bobby got up and walked over to see what it was. Sue opened it, looked at Bobby, then at Carol. "This is wonderful, Carol. I'm so proud of you."

Bobby said, "I knew you could do it."

Carol had gotten all As on her report card. Carol said with a smile, "I want my little sister to be proud of me. I want to be there for her."

"How do you know it's a little girl?" Sue asked.

"I had a dream last night about a girl and a dog. She told me I will have a sister, and I believe her." Carol said. Bobby said, "We will see soon," knowing Scout had visited Carol in her dreams.

* * *

Jessie and Mae were enjoying dinner in their first real home. Neither could believe how far they had come in a year. "Just think, Jessie, last year we were a stable boy and girl working for a man who controlled our lives. And now you have a good job, and we bought a house. How exciting is that!" Mae said with a smile on her face.

"It has been a crazy year. I will give you that. But I do like the outcome, and seeing you so happy is like icing on the cake." Jessie loved Mae very much.

Mae got up to go to the bathroom. When she came walking back into the kitchen, she had her overnight bag in her hand.

"Where are you going, Mae?" Jessie asked, because she was so calm.

"Water broke. Time to go to the hospital," Mae said with a smile.

"No way," Jessie said. "Time to put the cherry on the icing."

"What?" Mae asked.

"Never mind," Jessie said. "Let's go have a baby!" He was so excited. He was about to bust a gut.

* * *

Back a Bobby's house, Sue was arguing with Carol, telling her she had to go her grandparents. That was the plan.

"I want to go with you. I want to see my sister," Carol cried.

"I'll make you a deal, Carol. As soon as the baby is born, Dad will call Grandma, and she will bring you straight to the hospital to see your brother or sister. Will that work?" Sue was pleading because she knew she had to get to the hospital. Carol reluctantly got in her Grandma's car, rolled down the window, and said, "It's a girl." She rolled the window up and looked straight ahead because she was still pouting.

Lieutenant Glen, on the other hand, was having dinner at his house with a lady friend when the phone rang. He looked at his phone and saw it was his sister, Nancy. "I have to take this," he said to his friend. "It's my sister." He got up and walked into the other room. "Hello, Nancy, is everything OK?"

"Yes," Nancy said. "Everything is OK, but Vic insists on talking to you."

"I've never talked to him on the phone. Will he talk on the phone, or do I have to come over?" He didn't want to do that tonight. It was his first date to come to his house in a long time.

"No, no. He'll say what he has to say, and it will be over. But please let him tell you whatever it is so he will settle down." Nancy was a little frazzled.

"OK, put him on the phone. "Lieutenant Glen heard Vic's voice. "Hello, Adam. Hello."

"I'm here, Vic. What can I do for you?" Lieutenant Glen said calmly.

"You have to go to the hospital to see Willy and Scout. That's all. Good night," Vic said. Then he gave the phone back to his mom.

"Do you know what that means, Adam?" Nancy said.

"I think so. Tell Vic thank you." And Lieutenant Glen hung up the phone and went into the other room.

"I'm terribly sorry, but I need to go to the hospital. I think my friend is having a baby," Lieutenant Glen said trying to contain himself.

"I have to go to the hospital also. Seems that the maternity ward is filling up," the lady friend said.

"Would you like for me to give you a ride?" Lieutenant Glen asked.

"That would be nice. Thank you." Lieutenant Glen and his lady friend went out and got into his car and headed to the hospital.

Once there, he said, "Patty, I would be glad to give you a ride home later if you like."

"We'll see how long the night is. I will let you know. And thank you for dinner."

Lieutenant Glen let his lady friend out where the doctors and employees enter the hospital, then he went to park the car. He entered the front of the hospital and asked where the maternity ward was. The lady at the desk said, "Go around the corner. Take the elevator to the sixth floor. When you get off the elevator, to the left is the viewing room of the newborns, and to the right is the guest waiting room." Then she handed him a visitor card to pin on his shirt.

Lieutenant Glen entered the maternity ward waiting room and walked up to the information desk. A nice older lady was sitting there. She looked up. "Can I help you, sir?"

"Yes. I was looking to see if the McVeigh or the Carson family is here? They both are due to have babies," Lieutenant Glen said proudly." Did someone call you, sir?" the lady asked.

"No. Long story. But could you check to see if either are here, please." A door opened up on the other side of the room, and a man stuck his head out. It was Bobby.

"I figured you would be here. Vic, right?" Bobby said with a big smile. "How is it going? Sue doing OK?" Lieutenant Glen said, knowing it had to be fine since Bobby had that goofy grin on his face. "Yes, the babies are fine. They are cleaning everyone up, and they should be in the nursery soon. We'll be out their soon," Bobby said as he was fixing to walk back through the door. "Bobby, Sue had twins?" Lieutenant Glen was confused. "No, Mae had her baby at the same time Sue did. It was a crazy night. I will tell you all about it shortly." Then Bobby closed the door and was gone. The information lady turned around, looked at Lieutenant Glen, and said, "Yes, both those families are here now having their babies."

Lieutenant Glen thought, Really? You didn't just see or hear me talking to these people? All he could say was "Thank you." And he sat down.

It wasn't long before Bobby and Jessie came into the waiting room to find Lieutenant Glen. "Come on, Lieutenant. Come see the babies." Bobby and Jessie couldn't contain themselves. It felt good to be around so much happiness. "I'm coming. Can't wait to see them." Lieutenant Glen was getting caught up in the excitement.

As they were walking over to the viewing window for the nursery, the elevator doors open – and I stepped off.

"Scout!" all three said at the same time.

"I had to come see my new brother and sister, didn't I?" I said I couldn't wait to see them. We all walked over to the big window. There was a beautiful lady doctor who brought the two babies to the window for viewing. She looked up and saw Lieutenant Glen, and everyone saw a twinkle in her eye. After setting the babies in the viewing area, she walked away, and a nurse was standing by if needed.

"Scout, why is it that we are the only ones who can see you?" Lieutenant Glen asked.

"Everyone can see me. I just don't mean anything to them. You, Bobby, Jessie, and Mae let me into your hearts. When you love and care for someone, you will always be able to see them. That's how Grandma explains it. You don't remember everyone you see."

Everyone was focused on the babies now. I thought that they were the most amazing thing I had ever seen. I wanted to come see the babies but wasn't sure. Grandma said to go, and I'm glad she did. I had never seen a newborn baby. My heart just filled with something wonderful. I couldn't explain it, but it was good.

"Can I go see Mae, Jessie? I have something for her and Sue." "Yes, but Sue won't be able to see you. She doesn't remember you at all."

"It'll be OK. Where are their rooms?" "Room 625, just down that hallway. They're both in the same room, and they were asleep when I walked out," Bobby said.

"Boy, it's good to see you, Scout. You look good. Are you happy?" Bobby continued, "We all feel a little guilty about what had happened to you."

I gave Bobby a big hug and said, "I love you guys, and this is all for a purpose. I'm good. I love my new life and cannot wait till I can share it with you one day."

I headed down the hall to find Mae. I couldn't wait to see her.

When I walked into the room, Mae was just staring at the ceiling. Sue was fast asleep.

"Hello, Mae," I whispered.

"Scout! Oh Scout! It is so good to see you." Mae started crying. "We tried to find you, but we couldn't. Are you OK?"

I ran over and gave Mae a hug. "I love you, Mae, and I really miss you. But I'm good. I love my new life. But I had to come see my new sister and brother and, most of all, you." Mae was crying. "Stop crying. I brought you and Sue something, but this is special for you."

I pulled out a two cups with lids on them and put one beside Mae and the other beside Sue, who was still sleeping.

"What is this Scout?' Mae asked.

"Just some soup I made for you. It will make you feel better. Please try it," I reassured her.

Mae removed the lid from the cup and took a sip. She felt the soup go down in her stomach and then cover her body like a blanket. The smell from the soup was like a garden or green fields or just wonderful. Before Mae knew it, she had drunk all her soup, and she felt like she had never felt before. It was unbelievable.

"Scout, what is this soup?" Mae asked.

"Grandma's healing soup. But what I really want you to see is your cup. Read the side of it." I was getting excited. Mae looked at the cup. It had a dolphin and Edisto Island on it—made by Uncle Joe.

"Who is Uncle Joe, Scout?

"The man at the country store," I said. "Uncle Joe thought you were the prettiest lady he had ever seen, so he made this for you."

"So all that really happened?" Mae said, relieved. "Oh yes, and one day you will come back to the island but not yet. Grandma said that when that day comes, you can make the decision to stay if you want. But you will always be able to come visit. The time is not right yet. I have to go now. Make sure Sue drinks her soup. You both will feel like new in the morning. Love you. I will see you again soon." As I was walking out the door, Mae said, "Love you too, Scout."

Then I heard Sue wake up and say, "Mae, who in the world are you talking to?"

"No one. There is some soup on your tray. Try it. It's really good," Mae told her.

"Man, this is good," Sue said.

Scout walked back to the viewing window for the nursery, where the men were still staring at the babies. Lieutenant Glen was holding his back, like he was in pain.

"Lieutenant Glen, are you OK?" I asked.

"I'm OK, Scout, just lasting injuries from when I was in this hospital. The doctors want to do surgery. I keep putting it off," Lieutenant Glen said.

"You mind if I try something?" I asked Lieutenant Glen. Bobby and Jessie's attention now was on Lieutenant Glen and me.

"I guess it's OK," Lieutenant Glen said sheepishly.

"OK. Please chew on this." I pulled out one of the herbs that I had brought with me. "Now turn around and face the wall."

"Am I going to jail?" Lieutenant Glen was playing along as best as he could. But he did turn around and face the wall.

I ran my hands down his spine, then up again, till I found the spot. I handed him another herb and told him to bite down on it. Lieutenant Glen did as I asked. I reared back, and with my fist and good force, I punched him in the spot that was hurting him. Lieutenant Glen never moved. He finally turned around...and around...and walked down the hall...and turned around, then came back. Bobby and Jessie just watched, not sure what to say.

"How do you feel, Lieutenant?" Bobby finally asked.

"Like a new man. I cannot believe it. I love you, Scout." Lieutenant Glen couldn't believe he had no pain. Patty came walking down the hall. "Adam, I could use that ride home if the offer is still on the table."

Bobby looked at Jessie and said, "That's the doctor who delivered the babies."

Jessie said, "She sure is pretty. Look at the lieutenant. He's all giddy. Well, it's about time he had a lady friend."

"Well, I need to go also," I said. "So if you don't mind, I will ride down with you." I gave everyone a hug. So Lieutenant Glen, Patty, and I headed to the elevator.

As we were getting in the elevator, I looked back and asked, "What are my brother's and sister's names?"

Jessie called back, "Willy Jessie McVeigh."

Then Bobby said, with a big grin, "Leah Scout Carson."

The elevator doors closed—with new life and adventures in the future.

When the elevator doors opened on the ground floor, Patty and Lieutenant Glen stepped off.